CHARLIE BUMPERS vs.

THE SQUEAKING SKULL

To Samuel!

Bill Harley

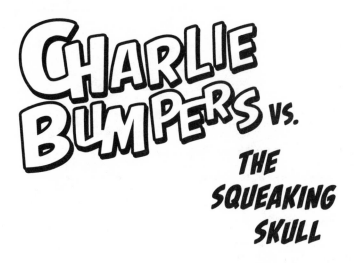

Bill Harley

Illustrated by Adam Gustavson

PEACHTREE
PUBLISHERS

Published by
PEACHTREE PUBLISHERS
1700 Chattahoochee Avenue
Atlanta, Georgia 30318-2112
www.peachtree-online.com

First trade paperback edition published in 2015

Design by Nicola Simmonds Carmack
Composition by Melanie McMahon Ives

The illustrations were rendered in India ink and watercolor.

Printed in June 2015 in the United States of America by RR Donnelly & Sons in Harrisonburg, VA
10 9 8 7 6 5 4 3 2 1 (hardcover)
10 9 8 7 6 5 4 3 2 1 (trade paperback)

Library of Congress Cataloging-in-Publication Data

Harley, Bill, 1954-
  Charlie Bumpers vs. the Squeaking Skull / by Bill Harley ; illustrated by Adam Gustavson.
    pages cm
ISBN 978-1-56145-808-0 (hardcover) 978-1-56145-888-2 (trade paperback)
  Summary: As Halloween nears, Charlie and Tommy hope to get out of taking their little sisters trick-or-treating and go by themselves to Alex's upscale neighborhood instead, then attend a sleepover at Alex's house, but when Charlie learns that partygoers will be watching a very scary horror movie he panics.
  [1. Halloween—Fiction. 2. Fear—Fiction. 3. Schools—Fiction. 4. Behavior—Fiction. 5. Family life—Fiction. 6. Humorous stories.] I. Gustavson, Adam, illustrator. II. Title. III. Title: Charlie Bumpers versus the Squeaking Skull.
  PZ7.H22655Crv 2014
  [Fic]—dc23
                                    2014006497

To my dad, Max Harley

Thanks to Jane Murphy, for her continued
careful reading and acute insight

Contents

1
Tons of Candy

"What are you wearing for Halloween?" Tommy yelled over the noise in the gym.

"I don't know," I said. There were only twelve days to Halloween, and I hadn't decided what I wanted to be.

Tommy Kasten's my best friend. We were leaning against the gym wall during recess, since it was raining too hard to go outside. There were two different kickball games going, a basketball game, and some kids skipping rope. With everyone yelling and screaming, Tommy and I could barely hear ourselves think. For a few minutes we watched everyone else run around.

Mr. Shuler, our gym teacher, was watching, too. I could tell by the look on his face that he didn't like all these kids crowded into his gym.

"Maybe I'll go as Mr. Shuler," I said. "That would be scary."

"Ha!" Tommy snorted. "I'm going as a werewolf. I've got some fangs to put in my mouth, and I'm going to glue hair all over my hands and face."

"Your mom's going to let you glue hair on yourself?" I asked.

"I hope so," Tommy said.

"That'll be great. I can't think of anything good to be this year."

"Well, you'd better figure something out pretty soon," he said. "Don't forget about the costume contest. The winner gets ten free movie tickets."

"I know." There was going to be a costume contest at school, and I wanted to win. Then Tommy and I could go to the movies five times together. Or maybe I would take someone else, too. Like Hector, who sits next to me in Mrs. Burke's fourth-grade class.

"Want to come to my house for trick-or-treating?" I asked.

"If I do, I'll have to bring Carla," Tommy said.

Carla is Tommy's little sister. She's in first grade, just like my sister Mabel, and they're best friends, too. My dad calls Mabel "Squirt," but I call her "the Squid" because it's funnier.

"I know," I said. "I always have to take the Squid around. We could do it together."

"I guess," Tommy said. "The only problem is Carla slows me down. I can never get to as many houses as I want. And when Mom or Dad comes with us, they stop and talk to the grown-ups handing out the candy. It's worse than going to the supermarket with them. It takes forever."

"Exactly!" I agreed.

"It's too bad we can't go by ourselves," Tommy said.

"And it's too bad we can't go to a neighborhood where the houses are really big and everyone hands out huge candy bars."

"Right!" said Tommy, getting more excited. "The bigger the houses, the bigger the candy bars! Then maybe we'd have to carry extra bags for when the first ones got filled up. That would be stupendous."

"Terrific!" I said.

"Stupific!" Tommy said.

"Stupific!" I repeated. "That's hilarious."

"Stupific!" we both crowed at the same time.

"Wait!" Tommy said. "Maybe your brother Matt could take Carla and Mabel around, and we could go to a different neighborhood by ourselves!"

"Maybe," I said. But I wondered if Matt would really take two first graders out trick-or-treating. Anyway, the Squid usually wanted to do things with me.

"Hey!" Alex MacLeod ran up, bouncing a ball a million miles an hour. He's a nice guy, but hyper— very, very hyper.

"What are you guys doing for Halloween?" Alex asked, still bouncing.

"Trick-or-treating," Tommy said. "Duh."

4

Alex lost the ball and ran to retrieve it. When he bounced it back our way, I caught it and held on to it. He didn't seem to notice.

"You wanna come to my house?" he asked. "I'm going to have a sleepover. We'll go out trick-or-treating in my neighborhood, then watch movies. It'll be great."

Tommy and I looked at each other. A dream come true. We knew where Alex lived—his house was really big, and his neighborhood was full of other big houses. Every one of them was probably loaded with giant candy bars.

Carla and Mabel the Squid wouldn't be there. Tons of candy! Heaven on earth on Halloween!

Tommy and I smiled at each other.

"Sure," I said.

"How many bags should we bring?" Tommy asked.

"As many as you want," Alex said. "It's going to be awesome. And I'm going to get some horror movies."

"I love scary movies," Tommy said.

"I hope we can get *The Shrieking Skull*," Alex said. "It's the scariest horror movie ever!"

"Fantastic!" Tommy said.

"Ask your parents if you can come," Alex said. "We'll eat candy and pizza until we throw up, and then watch scary movies and scream like crazy."

"Stupific!" Tommy said.

"Super stupific," I said.

Halloween with friends. Lots of candy. All of it *was* really stupific.

Except for one thing.

I HATE horror movies.

2

Maybe I Am a Dorky Chicken

I know I'm supposed to like scary movies—everyone talks about how great they are—but I don't.

One Friday night when I was in second grade, Matt talked our mom into letting us watch a scary movie together as a family. The Squid was only four and was already in bed. My dad wasn't really paying attention, and he fell asleep on the couch (as usual) right after the movie started.

The phone rang and my mom left the room to talk, and then it was just Matt and me watching the movie.

I was doing okay until this really creepy-looking guy started up the stairs to where the kids were all having a sleepover. The kids were acting like bozos and making a lot of noise, so they didn't hear him moaning outside their door. "I don't like this," I whispered to Matt.

"Shhhh," said Matt. "This is the best part."

"Does something bad happen?" I asked.

"Just be quiet and watch!"

I was getting really nervous. I wanted to tell the kids in the movie that something awful was going to happen. But they were laughing and acting like there was no such thing as a creepy-looking guy who wanted to get them all.

Like I said, they were bozos.

"I don't want to see this," I said.

"Shhhh!" Matt said again.

I squinched my eyes almost shut and hugged my pillow to my chest.

"Watch!" Matt said. "Don't be such a chicken!"

So I watched. I wished I hadn't.

When the creepy-looking guy's ax chopped through the door, I screamed so loud that Mom came back.

She turned off the movie and told us to go to bed. Matt complained that he should be allowed to watch the rest of it, but Mom said she didn't like us watching that kind of horror stuff and she didn't know why she even let Matt choose the movie to begin with.

Then Dad woke up and grumbled, "Everybody go to bed."

I was relieved. But Matt was disgusted. "Dorky chicken," he grumbled at me as we headed upstairs.

Maybe he was right. Maybe I am a dorky chicken.

I can't help it. I just don't like scary movies.

I really wanted to go to Alex's on Halloween to be with my friends.

But not with *The Shrieking Skull*.

3

Trickier Than I'd Thought

When I got home from school, I took our dog, Ginger, on her walk. After that I sat at the kitchen table and made myself some peanut butter and crackers.

The Squid came running in. "Guess what, Charlie?" she asked. "It's almost Halloween! I can't wait!"

"Uh-huh," I said. I didn't want to talk about Halloween with her. Not until I'd talked to Mom about going to Alex's.

"Aren't you excited?" she asked. "What's your costume? Have you even decided?" Sometimes the Squid just keeps asking questions. Once, when she was four, my dad counted how many questions she asked in a day. It was over five hundred.

"I don't know yet," I said.

"Will you go as a ghost?"

"No," I said. What a dumb idea.

"What about a pumpkin?"

"No!"

"What about a giant bug?"

"No, Mabel! Quit bugging me. You're the one who should be a bug."

"I can't be a bug," the Squid said, stuffing a cracker into her mouth. "I'm going as a bunch of grapes. But you'd better think of a costume, or you can't go trick-or-treating with me. Don't you want to go with me?"

"Not really," I said.

"You have to," she said. "It's what we always do."

"We don't always have to do it like that."

"What do you mean?" She gave me a suspicious look. Her mouth opened in a big O like she couldn't believe what I'd just said. Cracker crumbs fell out of her mouth onto her shirt.

"I don't know," I said. "We won't go out on Halloween together forever."

"We always go out together," she protested. "It's what we do."

I didn't say anything. Suddenly I realized that going to Alex's would be a lot trickier than I'd thought.

My mom was going to ask what we'd be doing there. If I told her about the scary movie, she'd say it wasn't a good idea.

Matt would find out and then he'd tease me about being a dorky chicken.

But worst of all, the Squid was going to be really upset about me not going with her. And then my parents would feel bad for her and make me feel bad, too.

I was going to have to be very careful.

After I finished my homework, I found my mom alone in the kitchen. She was cutting up some celery to put in the salad for dinner. It seemed like a good time to talk to her.

"Mom," I said, "do we always have to go trick-or-treating all together?"

"What do you mean?" she asked. She wasn't really listening hard yet, which was good.

"I mean I always have to go with Mabel."

"What's wrong with that?" The chopping slowed down a little.

I didn't want Mom to listen too closely, because then she would start to ask questions.

"Well, she's kind of slow, so we can't get around to as many houses as I want. And then when you or Dad come along, you talk to the grown-ups, and that slows us down even more."

She stopped cutting and looked up. Bad sign! I wished she would keep her mind mostly on the celery.

"Charlie, what is it you want to do?" she asked.

Uh-oh, I thought. *Here goes.* "I...um...I want to go with just my friends," I muttered.

Matt came into the kitchen. "Hey, when's dinner?" he asked.

"When the cook is done cooking," Mom grumbled.

I didn't want to talk with Matt in the room. But Mom went right on with her questions. "So you want to go trick-or-treating with just Tommy?"

"Sort of," I said.

"You can't go with just Tommy," Matt said. "You have to take Mabel."

"I always have to take Mabel," I said.

"That's because you're her older brother," Matt explained, like he was a teacher or something.

"So are you," I complained. "Why don't *you* take her?"

"Because this year I'm in charge of candy distribution. Plus, I'm going to dress up like a ghoul and sit on the front porch and scare kids."

"Really?" I asked.

"Yep," Matt said. "I'll scare them so bad they'll wet their pants."

"Matthew Bumpers!" Mom snapped. "You will not do that!"

"But, Mom!" Matt protested. "You said I could."

"I said you could hand out candy. I did *not* say you could scare children."

"It's Halloween!" Matt said. "The whole point of Halloween is to scare kids."

"What about me trick-or-treating with friends?" I asked.

"Who else do you want to come over?" Mom asked.

"Well—"

Just as I started to answer, the Squid skipped into the kitchen.

"—Alex invited me to come over to his house," I finished.

"And you would go trick-or-treating over there?" Mom asked.

"Yeah," I said. "Tommy's going, too."

The Squid stopped and stared at me. "What?" she asked.

"Nothing," I said.

"Your big brother Charlie doesn't want to go trick-or-treating with you," Matt said.

"What?" the Squid asked again. Her voice was getting higher and higher.

"That's not true," Mom said.

Just then, the back door opened. "Sorry I'm late," Dad said.

"Charlie isn't going trick-or-treating with me!" the Squid squealed.

"What else are you guys going to do at Alex's?" Matt asked.

"I don't know," I said. "I just want to go."

"You'd better be careful, Charlie," Matt warned. "I've heard there's a crazy guy in Alex's neighborhood who eats nine-year-olds."

"Matt!" Mom said.

"Shut up, Matt!" I shouted.

"Charlie!" Mom said.

"I don't want to go trick-or-treating by myself!" The Squid started to cry.

"Mabel!" Mom said.

"It's nice to be home," Dad said. "Is dinner ready?"

◆ ◆ ◆

"Charlie *has* to go out with me," the Squid said as soon as we sat down at the dinner table.

"Not yet! Not yet!" Dad said. "We're not arguing about anything until I eat something."

So we all ate something and calmed down a little.

Dad asked about our days, which he always does. When it was my turn, I decided to go for it. "Alex asked if I could come to his house for Halloween. Tommy and some other kids are going and I really want to go, too."

"Are Alex's parents going out with him and his friends?" Mom asked.

"I think so," I said. "I'm pretty sure."

"He doesn't know," Matt said.

"I'll call," Mom said.

"No! I mean, you don't have to call," I said.

Having parents call each other is almost always a bad idea. They could find out more information than they need and then they might say no.

"Fine," said Dad. "I'll call."

"No, Dad!" I said.

He grinned. "Then Mom will call."

"Mom, please. I *really* want to go," I said.

"Who will I go with?" the Squid whined. "I can't go by myself."

"Matt will take you," Dad said.

"Can't. I have an important job to do," said Matt. "I have to scare trick-or-treaters."

"What about me?" the Squid asked. She does not give up very easily. Like Dad says, my sister is persistent.

"If Charlie isn't here, then I'll go with you," Dad said.

"You don't have a costume. What will you wear?" the Squid asked.

"I don't know," Dad said. "Maybe I'll just go in my underwear."

"Daddy!" she screeched. "You can't do that!"

"Why not?" Dad tried to look very serious.

"Because!" she said. "You just can't. And you'll be cold."

"Dad in underwear is really scary," Matt said.

I laughed. But I was still worried about my mom talking to Alex's mom. "I really want to go." I figured it wouldn't hurt to say it one more time.

"I know that," Mom said. "We'll see."

Not a good answer. When a parent says that, it usually means, "I hope you forget."

I decided the best thing to do was to be quiet and hope for the best.

4

Good It's Not a Goat

In school the next day, it seemed like any time we weren't doing math or reading, someone was talking about Halloween. Even our art teacher, Ms. Bromley, was having us make Halloween masks.

Ms. Bromley isn't like any other teacher at our school. For one thing, you never know what she's going to look like. I usually don't pay any attention to what teachers wear, but with her you can't help noticing. Sometimes she puts a lot of sweaters or jackets or shirts over each other, with some kind of scarf around her neck. Her hair looks different just about every day. Once, she tied bits of it up with rubber bands in little spikes all over her head.

Very weird. But I kind of like it.

I like art class but I'm not very good at it—most of my projects end in disaster. Once I used too much glue on my collage and got some in Ms. Bromley's hair. Another time, I stepped on the clay I was supposed to be making into a bowl and left a trail all around the room. Ms. Bromley said it looked like Sasquatch had paid us a visit.

In art class that day, I was making a devil mask. I had made two horns from empty toilet paper rolls, but I couldn't get them to stick on the sides of the head. After using about half a roll of tape, I finally got them to stay on.

My mask didn't look like a devil—it looked like a goat.

To make it look more like a devil, I painted it red.

Then it looked like a red goat.

Hector was sitting next to me. He moved here last summer from Chile. He's good at art and was making a really cool mask. It had a scary man's face, but the nose and the ears were pointy like a dog's, and it had big sharp teeth and a big mouth. It was awesome. He looked over at my mask.

"Is that a goat?" he asked.

"No," I said. "It's supposed to be a devil."

"It's good it's not a goat," Hector said, "because I'm making *el chupacabra.*"

"Choopa what?" I asked. Hector speaks Spanish, so I figured it was a Spanish word. Whatever it was, it didn't sound like English to me.

Hector pronounced the word very slowly. "Chu…pa…ca…bra."

"What the heck is a chupacabra?"

"It is a terrible creature that eats goats and chickens and horses and pigs and maybe even cows."

That sounded pretty interesting.

VanGogh

"What does it mean in English?"

"Hmmm. I think it would mean 'sucker of goats.'"

"Sucker of goats? Goatsucker?" I laughed.

"Yeah." Hector smiled. "They say it sucks the blood out of animals."

"What's it look like?"

"This!" Hector said, holding up the mask. "Kind of like a dog. But no hair. And big. And scary."

"Is it real?" I said.

"I don't think so," said Hector. "But people in Chile tell stories about them like they're real."

"Do they come out at Halloween?"

Hector shook his head. "We don't have Halloween in Chile."

"No Halloween?"

"Not like here. But I thought it would make a scary mask."

"You should definitely wear it on Halloween. You'd be the only goatsucker in town."

"I don't know if I'll go out to trick-or-treat," he said.

"Why not?"

Hector shrugged. "My parents don't understand about Halloween. And I don't really know any kids around where I live."

"You should go!" I said. "You'll get free candy! It's really fun. You could go as the goatsucker!"

Hector smiled and shrugged. "Are you going out?"

"Yeah," I said. "I always go every year."

Hector nodded, then went back to putting teeth on his chupacabra.

But I was thinking about Hector and Halloween. No kid should stay at home on Halloween. Especially if he could be a goatsucker.

5

Watch Out for the Goatsucker!

The next day at lunch, Tommy and I sat at an empty table. Then Alex came bouncing over like a kangaroo and sat with us.

"Hey, you guys," he said. He plopped his tray down and his plastic fork bounced off onto the floor. When he leaned over to pick it up, he knocked over his milk carton.

"Did you ask your parents?" he asked, stuffing about half of his taco into his mouth.

"I did," Tommy said. "I think I can do it. But my sister Carla is upset because I usually go with her."

"Same with me!" I said. "But I'm hoping I can go. My mom's going to call your mom."

"Okay." Alex finished off his taco in a second huge gulp. I took a bite of the chicken salad sandwich my dad made. He's in charge of making lunches every morning before he goes to work.

"Hey, Alex," I said. "Is anyone else coming on Halloween?"

"Maybe. I asked Joey Alvarez."

"I was just wondering…"

"What?" Alex asked, cramming a handful of grapes into his mouth. The kid was a human garbage disposal.

"Do you think Hector could come?"

"Hector?" Alex asked.

"Yeah. He's never been trick-or-treating, so I thought it would be fun for him to go out with us," I said.

"He's never been trick-or-treating?" Alex asked. "Does he come from Mars?"

"No, Chile. You know that. He told me they don't have Halloween there."

"That's crazy," Tommy said. "I can't imagine not having Halloween. I'd hate that."

"Me too," I said. "But they do have this creature there that eats goats and cows and horses and stuff."

"Really?" Alex's eyes widened and he stood up. "Does it just eat them whole? What's it called?"

"I can't remember the Spanish word for it," I said, "but the word means 'goatsucker.'"

"Goatsucker? That is so cool!" Tommy switched to his TV announcer voice. *"Watch out for the goatsucker!"*

"I know," I said. "And Hector's making this cool mask of one."

"Oh, right. I saw that!" Alex said, hopping from one foot to the other. "It's super-looking."

"So do you think you could invite him to come with us on Halloween?" I asked.

"Yeah, I think so," Alex said. "I just have to make sure there won't be too many people. Kyle Curtis might come."

"Why?" Tommy asked.

"I don't know. He lives two houses down from us, and sometimes I play with him. My mom thinks we should include him."

I looked at Tommy and he frowned. Kyle was friends with Darren Thompson, who had made me nervous ever since he gave me a wedgie in second grade. And earlier this year when we were having a race to see who was the fastest runner in fourth grade, Hector beat him. Darren still blamed me for making him lose, because I had asked Hector to run. And Kyle was always on Darren's side.

"Counting you, that's just five kids," I said. "I still think it would be great for Hector to come."

"Okay, I'll ask my mom," Alex said. "Do you think he'll come as a goatsucker?"

"I don't know," I said. "Maybe."

"What's your costume?" Alex asked. "I'm going to be a ninja."

"I'm a werewolf," Tommy said. "I'm putting hair all over my face."

"Cool!" Alex said. "Your mom will let you do that?"

"I hope so," Tommy said.

Alex looked at me. "What about you?"

"I'm not sure yet," I said. "I'm working on it."

Just as we were finishing our lunch, Hector walked by to put his trash in the garbage can.

"Hey, Hector!" Alex said.

Hector stopped and looked at him. "Yes?"

"Are you really going to be a goatsucker for Halloween?"

At first Hector looked confused, then he glanced over at me and smiled. "Maybe," he said.

"What'd you say it is in Spanish?" I asked.

"*El chupacabra*," he said.

"Chu-pa-ca-bra!" Tommy said. "Awesome!"

"Stupific!" I said.

"Hey, Hector," Alex said. "Do you think you could come to my house on Halloween? I'll have to ask my mom first, but if it's okay with her, you could go out trick-or-treating with us."

"Maybe," said Hector.

I could tell he liked being invited. I sure hoped it would work out.

"And you could be that goatsucker thing!" Alex said.

"Chupacabra," Hector said again.

"Yeah! Chupacabra!" Alex repeated.

"Yes," Hector said.

"And we're going to watch a really scary movie," Alex said. "*The Shrieking Skull*. It'll be awesome."

"Okay!" Hector said.

Boogers. I had forgotten about the movie.

Now I had to worry about Kyle Curtis *and* that freaky skull.

6

Don't Say That!

I made it all the way through dinner that evening without saying anything about Halloween. Finally, after we'd finished washing the dishes, I heard my mom talking on the phone in the hall. I went out to listen, but she motioned for me to go away so I went back in the kitchen and stood by the door.

I could tell she was talking to Alex's mom. They were chatting about some new grocery store and how good the prices were. Grown-ups always spend a lot of time talking about things that don't really matter. I wondered when Mom would start talking about something really important, like me going to Alex's house.

She finally asked who else was going to be there on Halloween. Then she asked if Alex's mom needed any help. Then she asked what else we would do besides trick-or-treating.

She listened for a while, then said, "I'm a little concerned, because Charlie doesn't do well with scary movies."

OH NO! I thought. *Don't say that!* I stepped into the hallway and made a desperate face at Mom. *"I'm not scared!"* I whispered, shaking my head. *"Don't say that!"*

Then she said goodbye and hung up.

"Can I go?" I asked.

"Are you sure you really want to do this?"

"Of course, Mom! That's why I asked."

"I have to talk with Dad about it," she said. "Mrs. McLeod told me they're going to watch horror movies. You didn't mention that."

"I forgot," I said, although I didn't really.

"I know you don't like horror movies," she said.

"I do now!" I said. "I really do!"

Mom looked right through my eyes and into my brain. It's hard to make your mom believe something she knows isn't true.

"I mean I'm not scared like I was before," I explained.

"I asked Alex's mom to let me know what movies they're going to let you boys watch. I told her I hoped they'd make sure they aren't too scary."

"Mom! What if she tells Alex?"

I thought about it. If Kyle came and Alex told him I was scared of horror movies, Darren would be sure to find out, and he would never let me forget it.

"Charlie," Mom said. "There's nothing wrong with being scared. And besides, you don't have to do something just because your friends are doing it."

"I'm *not* scared," I insisted. "I really want to go. Can I please go?"

Mom shook her head a little and sighed. "All right. If Dad says okay, then okay," she said.

"Thanks." I crossed my fingers and waited while she went in and talked to Dad.

When I heard him say okay, I did a little happy dance in the hallway. Stupific!

I was psyched, but I decided to keep it a secret at home. I didn't want the Squid to be upset about me not going trick-or-treating with her, and I didn't want Matt to tease me about being scared.

But it's hard to keep a secret in our house.

7

The Squeaking Skull

I was in my room reading a book for school when Matt came in.

"Are you going to Alex's for Halloween?"

"I think so," I said.

"Are you going to watch a horror movie?"

"I don't know," I said. "Maybe."

"Which one?"

"I'm not sure," I said. "Alex said they might get *The Shrieking Skull*."

"*The Shrieking Skull*? That's the creepiest movie ever!"

"It is?"

"You're going to die of fear when you see that movie."

"What's it about?"

"It's this really scary story about a skull with no body. It flies around and eats everything. It's terrifying. You're going to wet your pants!"

"I am not!"

"You might! Even *I* was scared when I saw it."

"Really?"

"Yeah, it's got this part in it where the Shrieking Skull starts chattering its teeth and moaning, and then someone starts wailing, like 'Ohhh noooo, the Shrieking Skuuulll! Argghhhhhhh!'"

Matt held his throat and made gargling sounds like someone was strangling his guts out.

Suddenly, my bedroom door opened wide.

It was the Squid.

"Hey, you guys! What are you doing?"

"Nothing." I didn't want to talk about the Shrieking Skull in front of our sister. I looked at Matt and he nodded—he understood.

"You were talking about *something*!" she said. "What was it?"

37

"It was nothing, Mabel," Matt said. "Just some dumb thing your brother is doing."

"You *were* talking about something," she said, folding her arms across her chest and screwing up her mouth. "I heard you. And I know what it was!"

"What?" I asked.

"Someone was screaming because of a squeaking skull!" She nodded her head like she had caught us.

Matt and I burst out laughing.

"What's so funny about a squeaking skull?" she asked. "What does it do?"

I figured it was safe if everyone thought it was just a squeaking skull. "It squeaks," I said.

"Why? How does a skull squeak?"

"It just does," I said. "It has this really high-pitched squeak and it drives everybody crazy.

Eeeeeek! Eeeeeeeeek!" I made as high-pitched a squeak as I could.

The Squid giggled. "That's silly! A squeaking skull!"

"Eeeeeek! Eeeeeeeek!" I screeched.

The Squid turned and ran down the hall. "Mom, I'm a squeaking skull! Squeeeek! Squeeek!"

"Matt, please don't tell Mom or Dad about *The Shrieking Skull*," I said.

"I bet you wish it *was* a squeaking skull," he said, "and not a shrieking skull."

"No, I don't," I said, even though I did. A movie about a squeaking skull would be hilarious.

"Don't worry, little brother. It's okay even if it is a shrieking skull." Matt lowered his voice to a whisper. "Because I have a plan to save you. I'll be back at bedtime."

◆ ◆ ◆

Later that night, I got in bed and waited for my brother. I wondered what he had in mind this time. Matt's pretty smart, and his plans are mostly good, but sometimes he comes up with horrible ideas, like the time he got me to use laundry detergent to wash my hair.

I didn't have to wait long. He gave my door a little rap, then came in.

"Okay. What's your plan?" I asked.

"I'm going to de-scare you," he said.

"De-scare me? What's that?"

"I'm going to fix it so you won't be scared by anything," he said.

It sounded like a great idea. "How are you going to do that?"

"Every night until Halloween I'm going to tell you a terrifying story at bedtime. At first you'll be really scared, but every night you'll get a little less scared. By the time Halloween comes, when you watch a scary movie you'll just laugh."

"Really?" I said.

"Works every time," he said.

"When else have you done it?" I'd never heard of someone being de-scared.

"You're my first case," he said. "But I'm sure it'll work. When you see people being devoured by a flying skull, you'll laugh your head off."

I decided it was worth a try.

"Okay," I said. "Are we starting tonight?"

"No," Matt said. "We'll start soon. When you're not expecting it. The first night will be the worst."

Now I was getting the creeps. Matt could be pretty scary.

"Good night, Charlie von Bumpermeister," Matt said in a raspy Dracula voice.

"Good night," I said. "Um, thanks, Matt."

"Anytime, my little brother. Sleep well." He turned off the light and slowly closed the door.

I rolled over. I hoped the de-scaring would work. But when I shut my eyes, all I could think about were flying skulls and evil goatsucking monsters.

8

Umbrellas and Vampires

The next morning it was raining like crazy and the wind was blowing. The Squid and I finished breakfast and started getting ready to walk down to the bus stop.

"Hurry up," Mom said. "And don't forget to take your umbrellas."

"I love my umbrella," the Squid said.

"I'll wear my raincoat." I didn't want to carry an umbrella around. It seemed dorky.

"You can share mine," the Squid said.

"No thanks," I said. Her umbrella was bright yellow and had rainbows and pink frogs all over it.

"You'll get wet," she said.

"I love getting wet," I said. "Let's go."

We said goodbye to Mom and went out the front door.

As soon as we started down the steps, the wind smacked us in the face.

"I can't hold my umbrella," the Squid said. "It's blowing away."

"Here," I said, taking it from her. "I'll help." I held it over her head and we hurried toward the corner. There I was, holding a dumb yellow umbrella with rainbows and pink frogs all over it—exactly what I did *not* want to do. What a bozo.

By the time we got to the bus stop, the wind was blowing even harder and whipping the umbrella around.

"You have to hold it better," the Squid said. "I'm getting wet."

"I'm trying, Mabel," I said. "I'm not your servant, you know."

"But I'm getting really wet!" she whined.

Then, an enormous gust of wind pulled on the

umbrella and turned it inside out. It was all I could do to hold on so it wouldn't blow away.

"It's broken!" the Squid squealed.

"No, it's not. I can fix it." I pulled on the little metal spokes to get it back the way it was supposed to be. Then I heard something rip. Once I got it the right way around, I could see there was a rip all the way down one side of the umbrella.

Boogers.

"It's ruined!" I could see that the Squid was about to start crying. We were both getting drenched.

"I'm sorry, Mabel."

"It's my favorite umbrella!" she said.

It was her *only* umbrella, so of course it was her favorite. I didn't point that out. When the Squid is screaming, you can't really explain anything.

A few other kids showed up. Danny Fujita, who lives down the block, looked at the umbrella. It was ripped and ragged, and the wind nearly pulled it out of my hands again.

"Wow," he said. "It looks like a bat wing flapping around."

"It's not a bat," Mabel said. "It's an umbrella, and Charlie broke it."

"I did not!"

"Yes, you did. And it was my favorite."

I told her that Mom would know where to get another one just like this one but brand new. The Squid calmed down a little and then the bus came. She didn't want her favorite umbrella anymore, so I had to carry it. We got on the bus, both of us dripping and me holding a broken yellow umbrella with rainbows and pink frogs on it.

The Squid sat in the front of the bus and I headed toward the back, where I usually sit. When Tommy got on, he sat next to me.

"Is that *your* umbrella?" he asked. I could tell by the way he looked at it he was wondering why I was holding a yellow umbrella covered with rainbows and pink frogs.

"No," I said. "It's Mabel's. It ripped and now she doesn't want it. Look," I said, opening it up. "Doesn't it kind of look like a bat wing?"

"Yeah," said Tommy. "Or it could be a vampire wing, except for the color. And the rainbows. And the pink frogs."

That's when it hit me—the answer to all my problems.

Well, at least one of them.

"Yes!" I stood up and punched my fist in the air.

"What?"

"You're a genius! No, I'm a genius! We're both geniuses!"

"What are you talking about?" Tommy asked.

"I know what to be for Halloween! Look at this!"

I held out one arm with the ripped umbrella hanging underneath it. When I moved my arm up and down, the cloth and spokes folded and unfolded.

"It's a wing! See? I'll get my mom to sew these on a jacket or something and they'll look just like bat wings. I'll be a bat!"

"Outrageous!" Tommy said.

"Spectacular!" I said.

"Spectageous!" Tommy said.

"Super spectageous," I answered.

"But are you really going to be a bat with yellow wings that have rainbows and pink frogs on them?"

I laughed. "No. I'll just have to ruin another umbrella. I could win the costume contest at school with this idea."

"Stupific!" Tommy said.

"Hey, back there!" the bus driver called to us. "Sit down and be quiet!"

We did. But I was happy.

Deciding to be a bat is a great way to start any school day.

I had the costume on my mind all day long. My mom is good at making clothes and stuff and I figured it would be easy for her to make a bat costume for me. She can do just about anything.

I thought.

That night when I explained to my mom about the costume I wanted her to make, she just rested her head on her hand. I could tell she was trying to listen—her forehead wrinkled up like she was thinking—but she looked really tired.

"Hmm," she said finally. "That sounds kind of difficult to do, Charlie. Maybe we could find something a little easier."

"But, Mom," I pleaded, "this is a really good idea. I might be able to win the prize with—"

"It *is* a good idea," she said. "But tonight I have to fill out all these forms for work."

"But, Mom, what about my costume?" I asked.

"We'll see," she said.

Not a good sign. She hoped I would forget.

It looked like I might have to make the costume myself.

9

The Long-Fingered Man

The next day was Friday.

Only one week until Halloween, and still no costume!

Everybody in class talked about what they were going to wear. Sam Marchand told me about some kid who was going as a rhinoceros, which sounded like a winner. But I knew my idea was great, if I could only figure out how to do it.

I could have done something easier.

But I wanted to be a bat.

That night, our family played a board game together and watched a movie and then it was time for bed. After Mom and Dad said good night,

I turned off the lamp on my bedside table and snuggled down under the covers. Ginger curled up right by my bed like she usually did.

Just as I was drifting off to sleep, I heard my door creak open. Someone came over to my bed and grabbed my shoulder.

I kept my eyes shut.

"Hey," Matt said.

"What is it?" I said.

"Are you ready?"

"For what?"

"Your first de-scaring. We only have a week to get this done."

I wasn't sure I really wanted to be de-scared right then. "Maybe tomorrow morning," I said.

"No," Matt said. "You can't do it during the daytime. You have to do it at night when it's already a little bit scary."

"I'm kind of tired," I said, sitting up in my bed. "Will it take long?"

"Not tonight," he said. "We'll just start off with

a shorter, slightly scary story. They'll get scarier and longer as the week goes on, until finally they're absolutely bloodcurdling and terrifying."

I didn't like the sound of that, but maybe by then I would be de-scared enough not to care.

"Okay," I said. I reached over and turned on my lamp.

Matt switched it off again. "We need it nice and dark."

"Then I want Ginger up here on the bed to protect me."

"No!" Matt hissed. "You have to be alone for it to work!"

I lay back and pulled the covers up to my ears. "Okay," I said. "I'm ready, but hurry. And don't wake me up completely, or I'll have trouble falling asleep."

"All right," Matt said. "Here we go." He slid closer to me on the bed and lowered his voice. "Many years ago, there was this guy who lived over on Fernglade, and he—"

"Fernglade?" I said. "I know where that is. It's just a couple of blocks over, close to Tommy's."

"Exactly. That's where this happened. This guy lived all by himself and he never came out of his house unless he absolutely had to, because—"

"Wait," I said. I was really awake now. "Is this true? Are you just making this up?"

"Yes, it's true."

"Really?"

"Yes, the house is still there. It's painted white now, but when he lived in it, it was painted all black."

"I don't believe you," I said.

He shrugged. "All right. But you'd be a lot better off if you knew about this house in case you walk over there. Want me to go on?"

"Okay," I said, "but don't make it too much scarier."

"I'm just telling you what happened. So, there was this guy who lived all alone in the big black house and almost never came out. He was really, really thin. So thin that if he stood sideways he almost disappeared. You'd barely notice he was there, and he could sneak up on people without them—"

"Wait," I said. "I thought you said he never went outside."

"I said 'almost never.' And anyway, no one ever saw him go outside because he was so thin. And he was really quiet, too."

"Oh," I said. "Well, who was this guy?"

"I'll tell you if you'll just listen. His name was Simon Purslip."

"That's a weird name."

"He was a very weird guy. The most important thing about him was his hands. You see, they were not normal…"

Matt stopped talking. The room was dark but the door was open a little and some light from the hall was shining through the crack. I looked around for Ginger but couldn't see her. Matt was holding up his hands and slowly waggling his fingers. I wanted to shut my eyes, but I couldn't help looking. "Instead of five fingers on each hand," he whispered, "Simon

Purslip had six, and his index fingers were really long."

"How long?" I whispered.

He held up his index fingers and moved them back and forth in front of my face. "A foot long. *Twelve long inches.* And he would slide up to someone, ever so quietly, and he would take those long fingers and he would…WRAP THEM AROUND YOUR NECK!"

Matt reached over and grabbed ahold of my neck like he was going to strangle me.

"AAAAAAAAHHHHHH!" I screamed.

I jerked up, my heart pounding out of my chest, and knocked Matt off the bed. He hit his head against my nightstand and landed on the floor with a big thump. Ginger started barking.

"OWWW!" Matt yelled, but

then he started to laugh. "You should have seen the look on your face!"

"It's not funny!" I screeched.

The overhead light switched on. Dad was standing in the doorway. I was sitting up in bed clutching my pillow and Matt was rolling around on the floor, holding his head and laughing. Ginger was still barking.

"What in the name of Pete are you two goofballs doing?" Dad asked.

Neither of us answered. My brother was still crouched face-down on the floor, rocking back and forth, moaning and laughing at the same time.

"Matt, get out of Charlie's room and let him sleep. And Charlie, quit beating up your older brother. It's not nice."

"I'm not beating him up," I said. "He hit his head."

"Whatever," Dad said. "No more funny stuff or you're both in big trouble." Then he turned off the light and left.

Matt got up. Ginger came over and licked my face.

"I didn't like that," I said in the dark.

"Wait until tomorrow night," he said, still holding his head. "It will be even scarier."

10

Completely Creepy

When my mom hung up, she didn't look happy. I had been standing there for a long time, waiting for her to get off the phone. "Mom, can you help me with my costume?"

"What?" she asked, like she hadn't heard me.

"My costume! I told you about making me a bat costume. We only have a few days left until Halloween."

She shook her head. "Charlie, I don't know how much time I'll have. The agency just called and they're short on nurses. I'm going to have to work a couple of weeknights this week, and probably next weekend."

"On Halloween?"

"I hope not, but I can't promise anything."

"What about my costume?" I asked.

"Maybe we could pick something up at the store. Wouldn't you like that?"

When I was little I used to pester my mom about getting a costume from the store because I thought they were cooler. But not now. I would never win the contest with a store-bought costume.

"But you're going to help Mabel with hers," I said.

"Yes." I could tell by the frown on her face that she was feeling bad. "But that's easy. Making a bunch of grapes is just attaching purple balloons to a purple turtleneck. Your costume sounds kind of complicated."

"But, Mom!" I whined.

"I don't know, Charlie. I'll try to find some time. We'll see."

There was that answer again. *We'll see.*

"Okay," I said in a way to let her know that it wasn't okay.

◆ ◆ ◆

That night, Matt snuck into my room again and perched on the edge of my bed, holding a flashlight. He turned it on and shone it under his face, which made him look completely creepy. "Time for the next chapter in 'Simon Purslip, the Long-Fingered Man,'" he said, speaking in a low, raspy voice.

"No thanks," I said. "I don't think this—"

"Come on," he said. "Don't give up so soon. It just takes a little time. That was a good start last night, but you didn't even really hear the story. You freaked out before I could finish it."

"Okay," I muttered. "But no wrapping your hands around my neck."

"But that's what the Long-Fingered Man does," Matt said. "It's part of the story."

"Just tell me, don't do it. And turn off the flashlight."

"Sorry, it's part of the de-scaring process," Matt said. "Are you ready?"

"Sort of," I said.

"I told you that Simon Purslip lived alone. But he didn't always. Once, he was normal. He was married and he had a son. And he had a good job, working for a secret government organization that tracked bad guys."

"Was he skinny then?"

"No," Matt said. "Let me tell the story."

Ginger got up and walked out of the room. I guess she wanted to sleep.

"So," Matt went on, "one day his wife and his son, who was nine years old, went missing. One of the bad guys had kidnapped them. Simon asked the government people to look for them, but they wouldn't help. After a while, he quit his job. He began to get really weird and stayed in the house a lot. He got angrier and angrier, but in a quiet way."

I thought the idea of being angry in a quiet way was really disturbing. Who knew what an angry quiet guy might do?

Matt leaned really close to me. "Then, people started seeing him out at night, walking up and down the streets, like he was looking for someone."

I was definitely getting freaked out. "Is this almost over?" I asked again.

Matt moved the flashlight a little closer to his chin. "Not long after that," he whispered, "strange things started happening. This kid who was exactly nine years old was walking his dog one night, and just when he least expected it…AAAAAHHHH!"

Matt yelled really loud—right in my face.

I screamed bloody murder. "AAAAAAHHH!"

Matt started laughing. Ginger bounded in and started barking.

My heart was beating like crazy. "I didn't know

you were going to yell so loud," I said. "That wasn't funny!"

"It wasn't supposed to be funny. It was supposed to scare your pajamas off. Mission accomplished. You're almost cured."

Then he got up and walked out before Mom or Dad could catch him.

Stupid older brothers. I really couldn't tell if Matt was de-scaring me or just enjoying himself. I made Ginger get on the bed with me, then settled back on my pillow and shut my eyes tight. I hoped I wouldn't dream about the Long-Fingered Man. Or the Shrieking Skull. Or even the squeaking skull.

Or all of them together in one dream. Yikes.

11

She Loves Weird Stuff

On the way into school Monday morning, I talked to Tommy about my costume. "I've got this great idea, but I don't think my mom is going to help me."

"Bummer," said Tommy.

"Is your mom going to let you glue hair on your face?"

"I hope so," Tommy said. "But I might have to do it by myself."

I nodded. Moms usually didn't glue hair on their children's faces. Or make bat wings.

"I can't do the bat wings myself," I said. "I need someone who doesn't mind doing weird stuff and is good with costumes and things like that."

"You need a weird grown-up," Tommy agreed.

As soon as he said that, I knew who to ask. I looked at Tommy. His eyes were open wide and he had a big smile on his face. I could tell he was thinking the same thing. We both said it at the same time.

"Ms. Bromley!"

"Yeah!" Tommy said. "She'll help you."

"Fabulous!"

"Tremendous!" Tommy cackled.

"Tremabulous!" I said. "I'll ask her after lunch. She always hangs out in the art room during her free time."

"Stupific!" Tommy said.

I found Ms. Bromley sitting on the floor of her art room, surrounded by ripped-up pieces of paper. She seemed to be making some kind of collage. She was wearing these crazy tights—one leg was striped green and yellow and the other one was red with big black dots all over it. Her hair was pulled up in one big bunch so it looked like she had a purple fountain on top of her head.

Bizarro.

"Hey, Bumpers!" she said. Then she went back to gluing the scraps of paper onto a big poster.

"Ms. Bromley, could you help me? I have this great idea for a Halloween costume, but I don't know how to make it."

Her eyebrows rose up over the top of her funky glasses. "Ooooooh!" she said. "What's your idea?"

"I want to make a bat costume using broken old umbrellas for wings."

"That is so way cool!" she said.

I tried to imagine Mrs. Burke saying something was "so way cool." I couldn't.

"Did you think of it yourself?" Ms. Bromley asked.

I nodded.

"Good thinking, Bumpers!"

"But I can't figure out how to do it."

She jumped up and went over to her desk. Before I knew it, she was back with a notepad and some markers. "Okay. Tell me about it."

While I did my best to describe it to her, she sketched on the notepad. She tore off the first sheet and did another sketch. "Is this sort of what you had in mind?"

It was better than what I had imagined. But it looked even more complicated.

"I don't know if I can do this at home," I said. "My mom usually helps me, but she's kind of busy this week."

"Why don't you do it here?" she said. "We'll make a little corner in the room where you can work."

"Wow," I said. "Thanks, Ms. Bromley."

She scribbled something on the sketch and tore off the page. "Here's a list of things you should bring in tomorrow."

> old black sweatshirt or jacket
> broken black umbrella
> twist ties from garbage bags

I folded up the sheet of paper and put it in my pocket. As I was walking out the door, Ms. Bromley called, "Hey, Bumpers."

I turned back.

"This is strictly a DIY project, you know. DO IT YOURSELF. I'll be around, but you'll be doing all the work."

◆ ◆ ◆

That night at dinner, I could hardly wait to tell everyone about the costume. I was pretty proud that I'd figured out how to solve the problem myself. I had Ms. Bromley's sketch in my pocket so I could show everyone.

- old black sweatshirt
- broken black umbrella
- twist ties from garbage bags

Matt went first. Then Mom said Dad should go next, and he told us Mr. Grimaldi had actually said something nice to him. Mr.

Grimaldi's his new boss. Dad doesn't really like him.

Then the Squid went. Forever. First she told about how Brady Bernhart, this kid in her class who always used to bug me at recess, had stuck a marker in the pencil sharpener. Then she told how Mrs. Diaz had dressed up like a witch one Halloween and put her cat in a little gym bag and carried it around.

"Every time she went to someone's door, she opened the bag a little and the cat stuck her head out and meowed," the Squid said. "Meoooow! Isn't that funny?"

"That is completely hilarious," Dad said.

"How funny!" Mom said.

I remembered Mrs. Diaz telling that story when I was in first grade. I had told my parents about it then. But either they had forgotten or they were pretending to hear it for the first time.

"Okay, Charlie. You're next," Dad said. "What's new with you?"

"Well," I said, "I figured out my costume."

Mom frowned. I could tell she was worried since

she'd told me she couldn't help.

"What is it?" the Squid asked.

"He's going as himself," Matt said. "Absolutely bloodcurdling."

"Ha ha ha," I said. "Maybe I won't tell *you*."

"Forget your brother," Dad said. "What is it?

"Well, I'm going as a bat and—"

"Been there, done that," said Matt. "Dime a dozen."

Dad pointed a fork at Matt. "Would you like to be banished to your room for the rest of your life?"

"No," said Matt, "but—"

"Then let Charlie talk," Dad said.

Matt rolled his eyes. But he closed his mouth.

And then I thought about a TV show I'd seen on *Animal Planet*. It gave me an even better idea.

"Actually, I'm not going as any old bat. I'm going as a *rabid bat*."

Dad nearly choked on a bite of meatloaf.

Milk sprayed out of Matt's mouth.

Mom looked horrified.

Right then I knew it was a good idea.

"What's a rabbit bat?" the Squid asked.

Matt was cleaning up the milk, Dad was still coughing, and Mom was shaking her head.

"Not *rabbit*," I said. "*Rabid*. It means it has rabies."

"What are those? Are they like babies?"

Everyone else was still recovering. I was suddenly the expert on rabid bats. "It's a disease that animals get sometimes. It's really bad, and it makes them act crazy. They foam at the mouth."

The Squid turned to Mom. "Are you going to make Charlie a rabbit bat costume?"

I answered before Mom could feel bad. "No," I said. "Ms. Bromley said I could do it in art class. I just have to bring in the materials." I took out the sketch and held it up.

A smile spread across Mom's face. "Charlie, what a good idea! I could never have come up with a design like that!"

"I'm mostly going to do it myself," I said. "She'll just be there to help. I have to bring in the stuff to make the costume tomorrow. The most important part is the broken umbrella."

"Like mine with the rainbows and frogs!" the Squid chimed in.

"No, a black umbrella. I have to find one."

"I happen to have two broken black umbrellas in my car," Dad said. "I knew I shouldn't just throw them away."

"I want to be a bat!" the Squid said. "Only a *purple* one."

"One bat in a house is enough," Mom said.

"I agree," Dad said. "Anyway, you're already a bunch of grapes."

"I hate to admit it," said Matt. "But this is actually a pretty good idea. Maybe I'll use it, too."

"No way. It's my idea," I said. "Not yours. I'm

the *only* bat in the house. And I think the rabid bat might win the costume contest at school."

"Really?" asked the Squid.

"Really," I said. "I might just win the movie tickets."

"Do rabbit bats hop or fly?" the Squid asked.

Matt's stories about Simon Purslip were getting scarier and scarier. I didn't know if I was going to make it until Friday. If the de-scaring got much worse, maybe I'd have a heart attack and then I would be dead and I wouldn't have to go watch a movie about the stupid shrieking squeaking skull.

By now, the Long-Fingered Man was grabbing everybody—not just nine-year-old kids but also moms, dads, grandmothers, grandfathers, uncles, aunts, dogs, hamsters, and kittens. At a certain point, I knew the stories couldn't possibly be true. If they were, there would be nobody left in our town.

"I don't believe this," I said to him in the middle of the story about a pet shop owner. The Long-

Fingered Man had taken all the furry little animals from the shop, one by one.

"It doesn't matter if you believe me or not," Matt said in his disgusted older brother way. "It's true."

It drove me crazy. This is exactly what I hated about scary stories or movies or books or scary anything. You were almost 100 percent sure that they weren't true and that they were just dumb stories made up to scare you.

But there was always just that little bit left.

The teeny tiny part you couldn't be sure about.

And that was the part that scared my pants off.

12

Don't Tell Anyone

The next day in the lunchroom, I told the guys at our table about Ms. Bromley and my rabid bat costume.

"It sounds really great, Charlie," Joey said. "I think you might win the contest."

"Thanks," I said. "But, you guys, don't tell anyone, okay? I want to keep it a secret."

Tommy made them all raise their hands and swear they wouldn't tell another soul. He also made them promise not to glue hair on their faces, since that was *his* idea.

"Is your mom going to let you do that?" Joey asked.

"I think so," Tommy said.

A few minutes later, Kyle Curtis came over and sat down at the one seat left at our table. He usually sat with Darren and a couple of other kids from Tommy's class.

"Hi, Kyle," Tommy said.

"Hey," Kyle said. Then he turned to face Alex. "What movie are you gonna show at your house on Friday night? I hope it's something real scary and not one of those dumb kiddie movies."

"Don't worry," said Alex. "It'll be scary."

Tommy and Hector and I didn't say anything.

"Well, what movie?" Kyle asked.

"*The Shrieking Skull*," Alex said.

"Awesome," Kyle said. "Then I won't mind coming. I've seen it like a hundred times. I even have my own copy." He looked around the table at us. "Have all you guys seen it?"

"I *almost* saw it," Tommy said, "but then we didn't get to go."

"I saw it," Joey said. "It was pretty freaky."

"The special effects are super," said Kyle. "You know what it's about, right, Charlie?"

"Yeah," I said, "sort of. This skull that eats things."

"Everything it can find! It eats dogs and cats and bears and then it starts eating people—men, women, kids, babies. It has blood running down its mouth and everything. It's awesome."

"Cool," said Tommy. Hector didn't say anything. Neither did I.

The more I heard about the Shrieking Skull, the less I wanted to see the movie. I started thinking about a bloody skull that flies around eating people. Then I thought about the Long-Fingered Man who strangles people with his long index fingers. And then I imagined a screaming skull with long fingers sticking out of its ears.

I wasn't getting de-scared. I was getting *re-scared!*

Kyle looked at Hector. "What about you?" he asked.

Hector shrugged his shoulders. He didn't seem very scared at all.

"Have you seen it or not?" Kyle asked him.

"No," said Hector. "But it sounds a lot like the chupacabra to me."

"Me, too," said Joey.

"The what?"

"The chupacabra!" we all said at the same time.

Kyle looked at us. "What are you talking about?"

"The goatsucker!" we all said.

Kyle frowned and rolled his eyes. "You guys are weird. Well, I'll see you Friday night. If you're not too scared of the Shrieking Skull."

Then he got up and left.

When we were heading back to class, Tommy asked Alex, "Is Kyle really coming Friday night?"

Alex frowned. "Yeah, my mother told me to invite him because he lives on our street and it would be rude not to include him."

"Are we really going to watch *The Shrieking Skull*?" Tommy asked.

"I don't know for sure," Alex said, "but it'll be something really scary. It won't be any fun unless we freak ourselves out."

"Uh-huh," Tommy said. "Right."

As we walked down the hall, Alex skipped ahead.

Tommy looked at me. "It's probably a pretty dumb movie," he said. I think he had guessed how I felt about it.

"That's okay," I said. "I might not get that scared, since Matt is telling me stories about the Long-Fingered Man."

"The Long-Fingered Man? Who's that?" Hector asked.

I told them about Simon Purslip.

I grabbed Tommy around the neck and yelled, "Arrrrrggggggh!"

He laughed. So did Hector. "That's scarier than some old shrieking skull," Tommy said.

I wasn't so sure.

But I knew I wasn't totally de-scared yet.

13

One Serious Bat

Ms. Bromley told me she was going to be in her room after lunch. She said I could just come down there right away and work on my costume through recess.

I did not want to miss recess. I wanted to play soccer. But I just kept reminding myself of the movie tickets. I had decided I was going to take Tommy and Hector three times. There would be one ticket left over. Maybe I would even take the Squid to one. Or Matt.

I'd left all the things I'd brought in for my rabid bat costume in the corner Ms. Bromley had fixed up for me. She had set out everything else I needed—scissors, some special kind of tape, a glue called epoxy, this little puncher thing she called a grommet tool, and these little round things called grommets. She explained what I needed to do, and then she helped me mark the places for the holes on the sweatshirt and showed me how to use the grommet tool.

"Good luck, Bumpers," she said. "You can work while I have my lunch. Just shout if you need help."

Then she turned on some noisy dance music and sat at her desk eating a salad that smelled sort of funny.

I tried to follow all her directions. I had to cut the umbrella fabric just right, really close to the ribs of the umbrella. It was a very complicated process—trickier than anything I'd done before.

Ms. Bromley came over a couple of times to see how I was doing. She had to help me here and there, but mostly she just left me alone.

Toward the end of the period, she asked me if I was about finished.

"All done!" I said.

"Um, not quite, Bumpers. Look around."

All around me was a big mess. How did that happen?

"It's okay," she said. "I'll help."

I picked up the extra twist ties and grommets from the floor, and she started putting away the rest of the stuff I hadn't used. There were still some pieces left over from my dad's broken umbrella scattered around on the floor.

"Wait!" she said. "I've just had a spectacular brainstorm." She took two of the pointy parts of the umbrella with fabric on them and attached them to the back of the sweatshirt hood. "Bat ears," she said.

They looked great.

"Put it on," she said.

I slipped my arms into the sleeves of the sweatshirt. Ms. Bromley zipped up the front. I lifted my arms, and the umbrella sections opened up.

Holy moly! They looked exactly like bat wings.
It was perfect!

Well, almost perfect. One section was bigger than
the other, so I looked sort of lopsided. But I figured
a rabid bat was bound to be a little bit lopsided.

Ms. Bromley pulled the hood up over my head,
since I couldn't reach back with my bat
wings. She started laughing.

"That is awesome, dude," she
said. "You are one serious bat."

"One serious *rabid* bat," I said.

"That's even better," she said. "What are you going to use for the foaming mouth? Shaving cream?"

Genius idea! That's exactly what I was going to use. My dad had a can of shaving cream. I'd spray some around my mouth for rabid foam!

I nodded.

"You've got to see yourself in the mirror," she said. "I wish I had one here. You did a great job."

"Thanks, Ms. Bromley." I smiled. Those movie tickets were mine!

All I had to do now was figure out which movies I wanted to see.

14

The Final, Ultimate De-scaring of Charlie Bumpers

It was just three days to Halloween. Mom was working late like she'd told us. Matt started dinner and Dad finished cooking when he got home. When we'd cleared away the dishes after dinner, I put on my costume and showed everyone.

"It's the best costume ever, Charlie," the Squid said. "Next year I'm going to be a bat."

"Pretty good for someone who is a total klutz at art," Matt said.

"Not helpful, Matt," Dad said.

"I *said* it was pretty good!" Matt protested.

I ignored him. Matt was good at art, and I figured he probably would have done a better job. But I was the one who'd had the idea and I was the one who had made the costume.

After dinner, Matt showed me what he was planning for Halloween night. He had stuck a bunch of corn stalks up on the porch, along with a rickety old chair from the attic.

"I'm just going to sit in that chair, really still, like I'm a mannequin or a stuffed scarecrow, and leave the candy in the basket by the door. And if a little kid comes up with his parents, I'll just be a friendly ghoul and hand them some candy. But if it's someone like Jared, I'll slump there like I'm some kind of dummy. When he tries to take some candy, I'll jump up and scream my head off. He'll die of fright!"

It sounded hilarious. "I wish I could see that," I said.

"No way. You'll be wetting your pants over at Alex's. But not to worry, little brother. Tonight I will tell you the final chilling story of Simon Purslip, the Long-Fingered Man. Then *nothing* will scare you."

Uh-oh, I thought. *Maybe I should hide until after Matt goes to sleep.*

My mom got home just before the Squid's bedtime. The Squid wanted her to make the bunch of grapes costume right then.

"So it'll be ready!" she insisted.

"No, Mabel," Mom said. "We have to do it on Halloween day, so the balloons don't lose their air."

"I think we should do a practice one tonight," said the Squid, "so I can sleep with the balloons on. It will be very comfy sleeping on balloons."

But Mom said no.

Finally, I couldn't put my bedtime off any longer. I put on my pajamas and brushed my teeth and called out good night to everyone. I read for a while.

No Matt.

Maybe he had forgotten. Maybe he was really tired, too, and had gone to sleep early.

I read for ten more minutes, then turned off the light.

◆ ◆ ◆

"Chaarrrr-lie," a voice whispered through the half-open door. "Chaaaaaarrrlliieeeeee."

I looked up. The door slowly swung open. I could see shadows on the floor. They looked like two giant hands, each with a really long index finger. The fingers waggled back and forth.

"Cut it out, Matt," I said. "You are not the Long-Fingered Man."

"Noooooo," Matt whispered. "Because the Long-Fingered Man is deaaaaaaaaad. And I'm going to tell you how he died."

"Really?"

"Really," Matt said.

I was a little relieved that the Long-Fingered Man wasn't alive anymore. But I didn't want to hear how he died. Unfortunately, Matt slipped inside the room and sat on my bed. Ginger sat up and looked at Matt like *she* wanted to hear the story.

I knew it wasn't true. I knew Matt was just trying to scare me. I knew it was stupid.

But it still gave me the creeps.

"It was getting so bad that people were afraid to go out at night," Matt whispered. "The police department had most of their men searching for the Long-Fingered Man. One night a policeman noticed an old run-down house on Fernglade Avenue. There was a faint light moving around inside the dark house."

"Matt," I said. "Stop it. This is totally freaking me out."

"That's what it's supposed to do," he said. "This is the final, ultimate de-scaring of Charlie Bumpers."

I hid under the covers. Matt pulled them back and went on with the story. "So the policeman got out of the car, and he let out his dog—"

"He had a dog? A police dog?"

"Yes, dummy. He had a police dog because he was a policeman. And don't interrupt me again. The policeman and his dog crept up the stairs." Matt's voice got quieter and quieter. "When they came to the door, the cop knocked on it…" Matt rapped his knuckles on my bedside table.

I shivered. *I hate this!* I thought. *I hate being scared!*

"The door creaked opened slowly, and—"

Before Matt could do anything to me, I jumped at him and yelled, "AAAAARGGGH!"

Matt let out a scream and rolled off the bed. He hit his head on my nightstand again. Ginger jumped on top of him and started licking his face.

"You idiot!" he yelled at me. "You bozo! You moron! You idiot bozo moron!"

I started laughing.

I was so glad the Long-Fingered Man wasn't going to leap through the door to scare me or the policeman or the dog that I laughed harder and harder. I couldn't stop.

"You jerk!" Matt said.

Then the lights came on. My dad looked down at Matt rolling around on the floor.

"What in the name of all that's good in the world are you two boys doing this time?"

"Being de-scared," I said.

"Matt, get out," Dad said.

"Dad, your younger son is a bozo." Matt stood up and walked toward the door.

"You're lucky he's not a rabid bat," Dad said.

15

Some Kind of Evil Plan

On Wednesday at recess, Tommy waited for me outside with the soccer ball. Hector joined us, but before we could organize a game, Alex ran up.

"Hey, you guys," he said, gasping for breath.

"Hey," Tommy said.

"I, um…" Alex looked down at the ground and then at us, like he was trying to find the right words. "My mom, she said that she kind of… Well, she says we can watch a scary movie, but she's not going to get *The Shrieking Skull* for us."

Stupific! I thought, trying to look really disappointed.

"How come?" Tommy asked.

"She said one of her friends told her it was really bloody and gory, so we have to watch something else."

"That's okay with me," Hector said. "I don't care."

"I'm sorry," Alex said. "I told my mom you all wanted to see it, but she wouldn't listen to me. She said it was too scary. It's totally not fair! She hasn't even seen it!"

I wondered if it was because my mom called. "It's okay, Alex," I said in a sad sort of voice. But I meant it. It was REALLY okay!

"Don't worry about it," Tommy said. "We can—"

"You guys playing soccer?" Darren Thompson shouted. He and Kyle Curtis had appeared out of nowhere.

"We're going to," Tommy said.

"Hey, Alex," Kyle said. "I told Darren about your Halloween party. Do you think he could come?"

Alex opened his mouth and then closed it. His

eyes shifted around like he was a hamster in a cage looking for a way out. "I don't know," he said. "I guess I could ask, but...um...I think there are kind of too many people already. Hector's coming and that makes six of us and my mom's kind of freaking out."

"Are you sure?" Darren asked. "I'd really like to come."

Darren had a way of making people feel uncomfortable. When he was acting all friendly like this it always made me wonder if he had some kind of evil plan.

"I'm *pretty* sure," Alex said. He was having a hard time saying no.

"I am, too," I said. "Remember when my mom talked to your mom? Your mom told her there were too many people coming already."

My mom hadn't really said that, but I figured Alex could use some help.

Darren looked at me like he was going to strangle me. "Whatever," he said. "Who cares about a dumb

Halloween party? You guys will probably just do some stupid stuff anyway."

"At least we're watching a good movie," Kyle said. *The Shrieking Skull.*"

Alex and Tommy and Hector and I looked at each other.

Darren saw right away there was something wrong. "That's what I thought," he said. "You're too chicken to watch a real horror movie."

"That's not it," Alex said. "We all want to see it. But my mom won't get it for us, so we'll have to watch something else. But it'll be scary, too," he added.

"Yeah, right. *Real* scary, I'll bet." Darren turned to leave. "Come on, Kyle."

Before he walked away, Kyle leaned in toward Alex like he was telling him a big secret. "It'll be okay," he said. "I know a way we can still watch it."

"How?" Alex asked.

"I've got my own copy. I'll just bring it and we'll watch it when your parents go to bed."

"Um…okay," Alex said.

"Unless you guys really are too chicken," Kyle said.

"Kyle!" Darren called to him. "Come on!"

"We're *not* chicken," Alex said.

"Okay," Kyle said. "See you guys later."

We all stood looking at each other after he left.

"Why is Darren like that?" Hector asked.

"I don't know," I said.

"He's not very nice." Hector had this way of saying things very simply—like they were just true. "He'd better hope he doesn't meet a chupacabra."

16

Bats Don't Need to Shave

The night before Halloween, I did my homework and then got out my rabid bat costume and put it on. Standing in front of the bathroom mirror, raising and lowering my arms, I noticed that there was a little rip in one side of the sweatshirt where I had attached the bat wings, a twist tie had fallen off, and one of the metal pieces on the umbrella was bent. But I still looked really cool.

Then I remembered the rabid part. I needed shaving cream.

I wondered if Dad would mind if I borrowed his can of shaving cream for the day tomorrow. I figured it would be all right, but I wasn't sure. He'd probably think using shaving cream as rabid mouth foam was funny. He loves a good joke.

But he's also a grown-up, which can sometimes be a problem.

I decided I'd better ask.

I found him in the family room, sitting in the big chair, watching TV.

"Dad," I said.

"You want something," he said. "I can tell by your voice."

"Uh-huh."

"The keys to the car?"

This was my dad being funny.

"No," I said. "I can't drive."

"What do you want then?" He still had his eyes on the TV screen.

"I wanted to know if I could borrow your can of shaving cream tomorrow."

All of a sudden Dad started paying attention to me. "Shaving cream?" he asked.

"Yeah. For my costume."

"I thought you were a bat," he said. "Bats don't need to shave."

"I'm a *rabid* bat, remember? And rabid bats need to have foaming mouths, so…"

"Okay. But listen to me, Charlie. You keep the shaving cream in your bag until you need to use it. Then just squirt out a little bit and put the can right back in the bag. Do you understand?"

I nodded. "Sure, Dad," I said. "I'll be super careful."

"You'd better be," he said, "or both of us will be in trouble with a capital *T* with you-know-who."

He meant Mom. "Thanks, Dad!" I couldn't believe it.

"Don't let anyone else touch it."

"Okay," I said. "I promise."

"I must be insane," he said.

17

You Have to Have a Hairy Face

The minute I woke up, I remembered what day it was.

Halloween!

The costume contest and ten free movie tickets!

The sleepover at Alex's house and tons of candy! And…

I tried not to think about *The Shrieking Skull*. The Stupid Shrieking Squeaking Skull.

I got ready for school, and put everything I needed in my small duffle bag. My mom was already up, taping purple balloons to the Squid's purple turtleneck. She had a huge bunch of balloons. There hadn't been any blown-up balloons when I went to bed.

I thought about my mom getting up early and blowing up a million balloons.

"Did you do all those?" I asked her.

"Your dad helped."

The Squid tried on the shirt with the balloons attached. She looked completely ridiculous, sort of like a giant bag of purple marbles.

"I'm a bunch, I'm a bunch, I'm a bunch of grapes," she chanted, dancing around the room.

"Grapes don't dance," I said.

"Yes, they do," the Squid answered, like she was an expert on grapes.

Then Mom made her take the balloon shirt off, even though she wanted to wear it to school.

We weren't going on the bus. Mom had decided to drive us that morning because of our costumes. So did a lot of other parents. The line of cars to drop kids off in front of the school stretched all the way down the street.

In the hallway, everybody was carrying their costumes. There were a lot of normal ones—capes or superhero costumes or masks of different cartoon and television characters. I saw the kid with the rhinoceros head. It was pretty cool and I got a little worried that maybe he would win—but then I saw there was nothing else to the costume, just the head. Maybe the judges wouldn't consider that a complete costume.

Tommy ran up, holding out two hairy rubber hands. "How do you like my werewolf paws?" he asked.

"Stupific! What about the hair on your face?" I asked.

Tommy frowned. "My mom wouldn't let me do it. But I have a plan."

"What?" I asked. Tommy was usually a genius when it came to plans.

"I'm going to cut off some of my hair this afternoon, then I'll glue it on my face when we go out tonight."

"Really?" I said. "How are you going to make it stick?"

"I found a bottle of white glue in the kitchen junk drawer. I tried it on a small patch on my chin last night and it worked. If you're going to be a werewolf, you have to have a hairy face."

I looked at Tommy and shook my head. "Wow," I said.

"I'll need your help."

"Sure," I said. The plan sounded a little crazy, but when your best friend wants to be a werewolf, you help him be a werewolf.

The kids in our classroom were showing off their costumes. Samantha Grunsky was wearing big sunglasses and a long feathery sparkly scarf, pretending to be a rock singer. She didn't look like a rock singer—she looked like Samantha Grunsky wearing sunglasses and a long feathery sparkly scarf.

"What are you dressing up as?" she asked. She reached over and looked into my bag.

I jerked it away. "It's a surprise," I said.

"What is it?" she asked. "Are those bat wings?"

"Maybe," I said.

"There are a million bats," she said. "Everyone's done that before. I hope you're not thinking about winning the contest—to win you have to be something really special."

I rolled my eyes. I thought about telling her my bat had rabies and she might get them too if she wasn't careful, but I decided to wait. I didn't want to give away the secret of the shaving cream—a secret worth ten movie tickets.

18

Are You Allowed to Strangle Your Little Sister?

At one-thirty, Mrs. Burke gave up trying to teach us anything and had us get our costumes ready. I asked her if I could take mine into the restroom so I could look in the mirror and make sure I got the ears on right. Some other kids wanted to go the restroom, too. She said we could go three at a time.

"Five minutes max," she said. "Or I'll send the Burke patrol out after you."

Alex, Sam, and I got to go first.

There were a lot of boys from other grades in the bathroom, putting on their costumes. When I put on my sweatshirt with the wings and pulled up the hood to show the pointy bat ears, everybody stopped.

"Awesome!" Sam Marchand said. He was wrapping strips of sheets around himself to be a mummy.

"Wicked awesome!" said a kid from Ms. Lewis's class.

"That is the best," hooted Alex. He was dressed up like a ninja and jumping all around the bathroom, kicking at anything and anyone who was near him.

"You are *so* going to win," another boy said.

The rabid bat smiled. They hadn't even seen the shaving cream yet! I had stuffed the can in the front pocket of my sweatshirt. I planned on spraying it around my mouth at the last second.

Mrs. Burke knocked on the boys' room door. "Time, boys!"

We filed out of the bathroom, and when Mrs. Burke saw me, she broke into a huge smile.

"Charlie!" she said. "What a great costume! Where'd you get it?"

"I made it myself," I said.

She patted the rabid bat on the back. "That could be a winner," she said.

Stupific! I thought. Mrs. Burke was hard to impress.

After everyone had changed into their costumes, we all lined up in the hallway and headed down to the cafeteria. Classrooms were filing down the hall from all different directions, and everyone was dressed up. Lots of kids pointed at me—I kept flapping my arms to show the umbrella wings.

When we got to the doors of the cafeteria, I saw Ms. Bromley standing at the entrance. She was dressed entirely in orange and black. There was a stuffed black cat sewed onto one of her shoulders.

She had on an orange wig. Or maybe her hair was dyed orange—I couldn't tell.

As soon as she saw me, she gave me a huge smile. "Dude!" she said. She held up her hand to give me a high five. I lifted my arm as high as it would go.

I felt something rip.

I looked down—part of the umbrella section attached to my left sleeve had ripped off and left a long tear in the sweatshirt. My white undershirt was showing.

Ms. Bromley frowned. "Oh, rats!" she said. "I'll go get some tape." And she bounced off down the hall, the cat on her shoulder bouncing with her.

In the cafeteria, we lined up and sat down on the floor by classes, with the older kids in back. Being in fourth grade, we were very close to the back, with only the fifth graders behind us. I kept looking for Ms. Bromley to come back with the tape. My left wing was waving around, barely attached to my body.

When the cafeteria was almost full, the first graders came in. I saw Mrs. Diaz leading in her class. In the very front of the line was the Squid, with thirty purple balloons taped all over her shirt.

Right behind her was Brady Bernhart.

I almost choked when I saw him.

He was wearing a bat costume.

Exactly like mine.

How could that be?

Brady looked out over the crowd like he was searching for someone. Then he saw me.

"Charlie!" he yelled in his croaky voice. He flapped his bat wings. "I'm a bat, just like you!"

I couldn't believe it. Brady Bernhart had stolen my idea! How had he found out?

The Squid, covered in purple balloons, just stood there looking over at me with her hand over her mouth.

She must have told her whole class about my costume!

Are you allowed to strangle your little sister?

Mrs. Rotelli, the principal, came to the front and told everyone to sit down. Three grown-ups I didn't recognize were sitting at a long table to the side of the stage. Mrs. Rotelli introduced them and told us that they were the judges for the best costume. Then she told the classes to stand up one by one. Each kid walked across the room in front of the table, where all the judges could see them. The kindergartners went first, but I barely noticed them.

I was still hoping that people would realize my costume was special since I had made it myself. I looked around for Ms. Bromley.

I was pretty sure Brady Bernhart didn't have a can of shaving cream. I figured that was my only chance.

When Mrs. Diaz's class walked across, Brady Bernhart flapped his wings and ran around in circles, squeaking like a bat.

Everyone laughed and applauded.

"Charlie," Hector whispered, "he's wearing your costume."

"I know," I said. "I think my sister blabbed."

Hector squinted at me and shook his head. I guess he wasn't sure what I meant. "Blab" isn't a Spanish word.

"I mean she told her class about my costume idea."

"Oh." He frowned. "We need the chupacabra to come and eat that little bat."

"Do you think the chupacabra would do that?" I asked.

"*Sí*," Hector answered. "For sure."

When it was time for our class to go, we lined up along the side of the cafeteria. Our custodian Mr. Turchin, who was standing near the entrance, saw me.

"Charlie!" he said. "You make a fine bat."

"Thanks," I said.

He leaned against the wall to watch the parade.

In a minute it would be our turn to walk past the judges.

It was time for the shaving cream.

I turned toward the wall and took out the can. I pushed the button on top and foam came pouring out.

A lot of it.

Too much!

I put some on my face around my mouth, but I still had a lot on my hand. I spread just a little more on, but the foam seemed to be expanding. My whole face was getting covered. I looked around, trying to figure out what to do with the extra foam.

"What's that?" Alex was standing behind me.

"Shaving cream," I said.

"Awesome!" He reached out and took a big scoop of it out of my hand.

"Alex, no!" I said.

Before I could stop him, he had swiped some on his face. He tried to shake the rest of the foam off his hand and a white blob flew out onto the floor.

Mrs. Rotelli walked over to us. "What are you boys doing?" she asked. Her voice didn't sound as friendly as usual.

"It's shaving cream for my costume," I tried to explain. I started to stuff the can back in my pocket.

Mrs. Rotelli calmly took it out of my hands and turned to Mr. Turchin.

"Mr. Turchin," she said. "Do you have something to wipe off these boys' faces?"

He pulled out a rag from his pocket and handed it to Mrs. Rotelli.

Before I knew it, I didn't have any shaving cream on my face. And neither did Alex.

"But it's for my costume," I explained.

"Your costume is fine without shaving cream," she said. "You can get the can back when it's time to go home."

Then she walked back to where she had been standing.

Boogers.

While I was waiting to walk across, I swished the spit around in my mouth to make it into bubbles, hoping I would look rabid. But the slobber just dribbled down the side of my face and I couldn't even wipe it off because of my bat wings.

A couple of seconds before I was supposed to walk by the judges, Ms. Bromley showed up with a roll of tape. "Here, Bumpers," she whispered.

"It's okay," I said. I turned and walked past the judges. I flapped my wings. The one that had torn the sleeve of my sweatshirt just waggled in the air.

I wasn't a rabid bat.

I was a slobbering bat with a broken wing.

Tommy and Hector applauded.

Some kid in another first grade class said, "That looks like Brady's costume."

Brady Bernhart won the prize for the best costume.

When we filed out of the cafeteria to head back to our classrooms, Ms. Bromley was waiting by the door.

"Mrs. Burke," she said, "I need Charlie for a second."

Ms. Bromley put her hand on my shoulder and led me down the hallway to her classroom. When she got there, she made me take off the sweatshirt. She glued some fabric on it where the rip was, then reattached the wings.

"There you go," she said. "Now you can wear it tonight when you go out."

"Thanks," I said. It made me feel a little bit better.

I started to head out the door.

"Hey, Bumpers," she said. I turned and looked at her. "I'm sorry someone took your idea."

"So am I," I muttered.

"But it was still your idea," she said. "A good one. And you made the whole thing yourself."

19

Maldore, Deliverer of Justice

Mom picked us up after school. The Squid was already in the car when I got in. She was trying to hide behind a lot of purple balloons.

"How did everything go, Charlie?" Mom asked. "Did people like your costume?"

"No," I said.

I looked over at the Squid. Her bottom lip was quivering.

"Why not?"

"Because someone else was wearing a costume just like mine," I said.

"That's impossible!" Mom said. "Who else would have thought of a rabid bat?"

I gave the Squid a dirty look.

"I didn't know!" she whimpered.

Mom looked at both of us in the rearview mirror. "Didn't know what?" she asked. "What happened?"

"I didn't know Brady Bernhart would be a bat!" the Squid squeaked. She was upset, which was weird, since I was the one who lost the contest because *some bozo* let out the secret so *someone* could steal my costume.

"Brady made a costume like Charlie's?" Mom asked.

"Yeah," I said, "because Mabel told everyone about it."

"Brady's mom made the costume!" The Squid's eyes were filling up with tears. "I didn't know that would happen!"

"Oh, forget it." I looked out the window.

"Now Charlie will *never* go trick-or-treating with me!" she wailed. She sniffed a big wet sniff and rubbed her face with a balloon. "It's not fair."

Mom didn't say anything. It was a quiet car ride home.

◆ ◆ ◆

Matt spent the whole afternoon setting up the front porch. At first he said he wanted to do it all himself, but when he heard about the bat costume disaster, he asked me to help string up the spiderwebs. We stretched fake webs back and forth across the porch. Matt let me climb up on the ladder to hang plastic spiders down from the ceiling on strings. He took his little speakers from his room and set them up in the window and started playing spooky music and screams. Then he put the old chair from the attic beside the door.

"Here's where Maldore, Deliverer of Justice, is going to sit," he said.

"Who's that?" I asked.

"Someone I just made up," he said.

"Is Mom really going to let you scare people?" I asked.

"Maldore, Deliverer of Justice, only scares people

who deserve it. Watch this." He reached into his back pocket and pulled out a kind of hood. When he put it over his head, his face was completely hidden by some black fabric. He looked terrifying.

"Can you see anything from under there?" I asked.

Matt lunged out and grabbed me around my neck.

"AAAAAAAAAAAH!" I screamed.

"Mwa-ha-ha-ha," my brother cackled. "Maldore administers justice."

I rubbed my neck. I guessed Matt was going to have fun without going out for candy.

Mom and Dad came home sooner than usual so we could have an early dinner. Dad planned to take the Squid around right after we ate, and Mom was supposed to have me at Alex's house at 6:30. I was so nervous and excited I couldn't eat much.

I asked to be excused so I could get my costume on and my overnight bag ready. Just as Mom and I were

heading out the kitchen door to get in the car, the front doorbell rang. Matt grabbed his hood and pulled it over his head.

"No, Matt!" Mom said. "Don't put that on yet. It's probably little kids. It's really early."

"Mom!" Matt moaned.

"Take it off!" she said.

"Dad," Matt said, pulling off the hood. "Tell her it's Halloween! People are supposed to be scared."

"You're scary enough," Dad said. "No terrorizing until Mom gets home. She's a nurse, so she can revive anyone who passes out."

Matt rolled his eyes.

"I mean it," Mom said.

"Okay, okay," Matt muttered.

"But you guys just don't get it." Then he went to hand out candy at the front door.

Mom and I went out the kitchen door. The Squid stood there watching us go.

"Charlie," she said.

"Yeah?"

"I didn't mean for Brady to be a bat."

"I know," I said. I wasn't thinking about that anymore.

"I really didn't mean it," she said.

"I know, Squid. It's okay."

"Maybe you could go trick-or-treating with me just a little?"

"Come on, Charlie," Mom called from the back door. "We're going to be late and I have to get back before Matt scares a three-year-old."

We went down the porch stairs and got in the car. As we turned onto our street, I saw Dad leading the Squid down the driveway. He was wearing a bandana over the top of his head and had a patch over one eye. It was good he wasn't in just his underwear. My sister was bouncing up and down like a bunch of hyperactive grapes. Matt was handing out candy to some kid dressed up like a pumpkin.

I kind of wished I was going with Dad and the Squid, or helping Maldore, Deliverer of Justice.

20

Hairy Rabid Bat!

Alex lives in a big house, and the houses around it are all big. They also have big yards.

As we drove down his street, it was the first time I'd thought about the problem of big houses and big yards. You had to walk a long way just to get from one house to another.

When we pulled into Alex's driveway, Hector's father was standing by the front door talking to Alex's dad. Hector's dad smiled when he saw me—I think he knew I was Hector's friend.

Hector had his chupacabra mask under his arm, ready to put on. Other than that, he was just wearing jeans and a jacket. But the mask was so great it didn't really matter.

Hector followed me into the living room, where Alex and Joey were waiting. Alex was even more hyper than usual, whirling around in his ninja outfit. Joey was dressed up as Buck Meson, Detective from Andromeda, my favorite superhero.

I gave Joey a high five and said "I DON'T THINK SO!" just like Buck Meson always says on the TV show.

Then Kyle came in carrying this big rubber mask of a guy with a hatchet stuck in his skull. It was the kind that covers your whole head. It was pretty amazing.

My mom would never have allowed me to walk around with a hatchet in my head.

Kyle was also carrying a shopping bag, which he put behind a chair in Alex's living room. "For later," he whispered. *The Shrieking Skull.*

Oh great, I thought. I was kind of hoping the Shrieking Skull wouldn't come.

Tommy showed up last, dressed in his werewolf outfit, holding his hairy hands. He had a stocking cap on his head.

"Where's the hair?" I asked.

He held up a paper bag. "In here," he said. "Hey, Alex. Where's the bathroom? I need to finish my costume. Charlie, could you come help me?"

Alex pointed to a door down the hallway.

Tommy and I went inside and shut the door. Tommy reached in the bag and pulled out a plastic bottle of white glue.

"Here," he said. "Squeeze out a little bit on your fingers and put it on my face, and I'll stick the hair on where I want it."

I looked in the bag. There was a pile of curly hair in the bottom. "Where'd you get all this?"

Tommy took off his stocking cap.

"Wow," I said. He had cut off a lot of his hair. There were some places where it was almost down to his scalp.

"Did your mom see this?" I asked.

He shook his head. "No way. I'll have to wear this cap for a few days so she doesn't find out."

"You are insane," I said.

"Come on and help me with the glue," he said. "We gotta hurry."

"Are you sure about this?"

"It's just glue. I can peel it off when we get back."

"Okay," I said. For just a split second, I wondered if this was a good idea. But Tommy was my friend. And I had done dumber things with his help.

I started spreading glue on his face.

"All the way up to the ears, and on my forehead," he said.

"How about your neck?" I asked.

"Okay, there, too," he said. "Werewolves are hairy all over."

As soon as I finished, Tommy took a handful of hair and stuck it on his face where the glue was.

"Stupific!" I said. "It looks awesome."

"Wow," Tommy said. "This stuff is really sticking to my fingers."

When he rubbed his fingers on his shirt, the hair stuck to it. I tried to help, but then the hair stuck on my fingers.

"Hey, there's still a couple of empty places," Tommy said, pointing to his cheeks.

I put some more glue on, but I used a little too much and it started to drip down. I stuck on more hair.

Some of it got in his mouth.

"Uck! Hairy mouth!" he said.

I laughed. I wiped my hands on my sweatshirt and got some hair on the umbrella wings.

"Ooooooooh!" Tommy said. "Hairy bat!"

"Okay, now I have to finish my costume." I took the can of shaving cream out of my pocket. "Hairy rabid bat!' I said.

I squirted some shaving cream into my hand. It came out really fast, into a big mound. I dabbed it on around my mouth the best I could, then tried to shake the rest off into the sink. Tommy started laughing really hard.

I looked in the mirror. My dad was right. I didn't look like a rabid bat. I looked more like a bat that was about to shave.

Alex's dad knocked on the door. "Come on, guys. Let's get going."

I looked at Tommy. Ready or not, it was time to go. We looked at the sink—it was covered in hair and glue and shaving cream. Tommy grabbed a wad of toilet paper and started wiping, but it just got wet and sticky and made things worse. We turned the faucet on and tried to clean it up. I used the hand towel by the sink to mop up as much of the mess as I could.

When we came out of the bathroom, Alex's dad was standing in the hallway. I was thinking about saying something to him about the sink, but then Tommy turned off the bathroom light and shut the door, so I figured we could tell him later.

Alex's dad stared at us. I could tell by the look on his face he was pretty horrified by what he saw.

"I'm a werewolf," Tommy said.

"I'm a rabid bat," I said.

"Oh," Alex's dad said, which is the only thing you can say when you meet a hairy werewolf and rabid bat coming out of your bathroom.

21

Teeny Tiny Candy Bars

As soon as we got outside, Alex started running up and down the driveway doing ninja kicks and falling over and jumping back up.

"Alex, let's stay together!" his dad said.

Alex wasn't listening.

I was thinking that if Mrs. Burke was here, everything would be a lot more organized.

It only took us a few minutes to get to the first house. We hurried up the driveway and onto the walk. Tommy was on one side of me and Hector was on the other side.

I wasn't worried about *The Shrieking Skull* right now. I was with my two best friends, who looked really great as a werewolf and a chupacabra, and I was going to get candy.

Tons of candy.

Three little kids were coming down the walk from the house with their parents.

"Hey, Jeff," Alex's dad said to one of the grown-ups.

"Hey, Kevin," the man answered back. "Been out long?"

Alex's dad stopped on the walk and started to talk.

Oh no! Parents were the same all over. Even in the big houses!

"Dad!" Alex said. "Come on!"

"You boys go on ahead," his dad said. Then he kept talking.

We ran up the rest of the walk. Alex rang the doorbell. Twice.

The door opened.

"Trick or treat!" we all yelled.

Tommy howled. Alex kicked like a ninja.

"Well, well," said the woman in the doorway. "What a scary group of monsters we've got here. What are you all dressed up as?"

"Ninja!" Alex yelled.

"Dead guy," Kyle said.

"Werewolf," Tommy said.

"Buck Meson, Detective from Andromeda," Joey said.

"Chupacabra!" Hector said.

The woman looked confused.

"Goatsucker!" we all yelled.

She still looked confused. Then she looked at me. "And what are you?"

"A rabid bat!" I said.

"Oh," she said. "You look kind of like a bat that's about to shave."

Boogers.

She held out a basket of candies. "Everybody take one," she said.

I looked into the basket. I couldn't believe it.

All I saw were teeny tiny candy bars, and she only wanted us to take one each. Where were the big candy bars that matched the big house?

We headed back down toward the street. It seemed like a long way to the house next door. "Dad!" Alex yelled. "Let's go!"

"Just a minute," he called. He was still talking to Jeff, or whatever his name was.

We went up and down Alex's street. Not one single house gave out big candy bars. No one let us take as much as we wanted.

We turned off of Alex's street and went down the next one.

One of my wings came unhooked. I tried to put it back on, but I gave up and clamped it under my arm.

"This hair is really getting itchy," Tommy said. "Especially around my neck. And the glue is so stiff I can't move my face."

"You can take it off when we get back to Alex's," I said.

But Hector was having a great time. "This is really cool," he said. "I can't believe people just give you all this candy. People who don't even know you!"

He was one happy chupacabra.

I couldn't help thinking a little about my neighborhood. And Matt scaring people. And even the Squid.

By the time we got to the end of the second block, everyone was slowing down. Except for Alex. I think he'd been eating his candy as he went along.

"Okay, boys. It's time to head back now," Alex's dad said.

"Not yet, Dad," Alex said. "We just started. I want to do a hundred houses."

That was a lot of houses. We'd done about twenty so far. If we were going to do a hundred houses, we'd have to stay out until four in the morning.

"No, Alex," his dad said. "I think we've done enough."

"Daaaaaad!" Alex whined. "Just *one* more street."

"One more *house*," his dad said.

"Three more houses," Alex said.

"Okay," his dad said. "Three more. But after that we go home."

I looked in my bag. The candy barely covered the bottom. I wanted more candy, but I was tired of walking around.

We did three more houses. One house let us have two pieces of candy. It seemed like a miracle. Who knew that big houses had so little candy?

22

Your Dumb Squeaking Skull

We dragged ourselves back to Alex's house. My loose wing had come off completely, and my mouth was filled with the taste of soap, which I kept spitting out.

"This glue is killing me," Tommy said. "I'm itching to death and my face is paralyzed."

Buck Meson wasn't shooting anyone with electron stares. Kyle was carrying the head with the hatchet in it under his arm.

Hector still had his mask on. The chupacabra was enjoying himself.

Alex's dad was walking behind us.

"I guess we didn't need two bags," Tommy said to me.

"Barely one," I answered.

Kyle said, "Well, at least we're going to watch a great movie. It's awesome."

I looked at Alex, wondering if he'd told his parents about Kyle bringing *The Shrieking Skull*. I doubted it.

"Are we really gonna watch the Shrieking Skull movie?" Tommy asked.

"Sure," said Kyle. "Why not? Right, Alex?"

Alex didn't say anything.

"We *can* watch it, right?" Kyle said.

"My mom got us a movie," Alex said. "So I think we have to watch that one first."

"What is it?" Kyle asked.

"*Space Gremlins*," Alex said.

"*Space Gremlins*?" Kyle made a face. "I saw that when I was seven! It's stupid."

"I saw it, too," Joey said.

"So did
I." I'd seen
it when I was
in third grade,
and I'd liked it. I was thinking
that watching *Space Gremlins* was
a very good idea.

The chupacabra was silent.

"Well, we have to watch the movie my mom
got first," Alex said.

"All right," said Kyle. "And we can watch *The
Shrieking Skull* when your parents go to bed. It'll be
better to watch it later anyway."

"Okay," said Alex.

Boogers. It sounded like the Shrieking Skull was
going to visit me whether I liked it or not.

"Before we watch any more movies," Tommy
said, "Charlie should tell his story."

I looked at him. I was surprised he'd said that.

"What story is that?" Alex asked.

"It's this really scary story and it's true," Tommy said. "He told me about it."

"Who cares?" Kyle said. "I don't think Charlie even wants to see *The Shrieking Skull*."

"Yes, I do," I said.

"No, you don't," he said. "You're afraid."

"I'm not afraid of your dumb Squeaking Skull!" I said by mistake. As soon as I said it, everybody laughed—Alex, Joey, Tommy, and even Hector, who still had his chupacabra mask on.

Except for Kyle. "Well," he said, "we'll see which is scarier. *The Shrieking Skull* or your dumb story about whatever."

"The Long-Fingered Man," I said.

"Wow," said Joey. "That sounds cool."

"And it's true," Tommy said.

"Really?" Everyone looked at me.

"My brother says it is," I said.

"Yeah, right," said Kyle.

We walked up the driveway to Alex's house. Inside, we took off our costumes. Hector finally took off his chupacabra mask. Tommy went into the bathroom and tried to get the hair off his face, but when he came back out, there were still big patches of hairy glue where he hadn't been able to peel it off.

"My face is killing me," he said.

"It's killing me, too," I said. Everyone laughed.

We poured our candy out on the floor.

It wasn't very much.

But Alex's mom called us into the kitchen, where there were three whole pizzas waiting for us. We sat down at the table and started eating.

"Now," Hector said, "I am not the goatsucker. I am the pizza sucker."

"We're all pizza suckers!" Tommy shouted. We all laughed and sucked pieces of pizza into our mouths. I wished we could just keep eating pizza until it was time to fall asleep.

We went into the family room and rolled out our sleeping bags on the floor. I put my bag between Tommy's and Hector's. Alex's mom started the movie. "I hope this isn't too scary for you guys," she said.

"It's fine," Joey said. "I saw it before."

"It's not scary at all," Kyle said.

"Okay," she said. "Watch the movie, then brush your teeth. And don't stay up too late."

We all said okay and watched her go upstairs.

23

The Attack of the Chupacabra

There were a few scary spots in *Space Gremlins*, but the story was mostly funny. Kyle kept saying how stupid it was. By the time the movie was over, we were all really tired. I just wanted to go to sleep. But Kyle insisted on watching *The Shrieking Skull*.

"If my parents hear it and come down," Alex said, "we'll get in trouble."

"I'll turn it down low," Kyle said. I could tell he wasn't going to give up.

"Wait," Tommy said. "First we have to hear Charlie's story."

"I don't want to hear Charlie's dumb story," Kyle said. "I want to watch my movie."

Kyle was taking over the whole sleepover. It seems like if you're bossy enough, you can get your way even if other people don't want to do what you want to do.

"No," said Tommy. "First let's hear the story. It's really good." He looked at me and smiled.

Tommy's nuts.

Hector spoke up. "I want to hear the story."

"Me, too," said Alex, "and it's *my* party."

"Okay," Kyle said, "we'll hear your dumb story. Then it's *The Shrieking Skull*—"

"Story first," Tommy said. "Charlie, you sit up there in front of us."

Everybody climbed into their sleeping bags. Tommy turned out the lights.

I got up in front of the television and sat down on the floor. The other boys scooched their bags in closer.

"Wait, Charlie," Alex said. He jumped up and

ran into the kitchen and was back in five seconds with a flashlight. "Use this! Put it under your face."

Just like Matt! I turned it on and held it under my face.

"Awesome," Alex said. "Now go ahead."

"Yeah, hurry up," Kyle muttered.

I took a deep breath. I tried to pretend like I was Matt sitting on the edge of my bed, waiting to scare me.

But this time I was the one doing the scaring. I just hoped I'd been de-scared enough to be scary myself.

"Okay," I said. "Do you guys know where Fernglade Avenue is?"

"Uh-huh," said Alex.

"I do," said Joey. "It's about five blocks from me."

"Right," I said. "It's close to Tommy's street."

"I walk by it almost every day," Tommy said. "It's a dead-end."

"Right," I said. "Well, down at the end of the block, there's this big house, way far away from the street. The grass is really tall because—"

"What's the address?" Kyle asked. I could tell he was trying to trip me up.

"There's no number on the house," I said. "And...um...there's no mailbox."

"Wow," Alex said.

"And the house is really old." I was trying to put in everything that Matt had told me. "And it looks like it's empty. But sometimes, if you're standing on the street really late at night, you can see a small light passing from one room to another." I lowered my voice. "They say it's the ghost of Simon Purslip, the Long-Fingered Man."

"Who?" Joey asked. There was a dim light on in the hallway, and I could see that he was clutching the edge of his sleeping bag and chewing on it.

Kyle took a quick glance at me and looked back down at the floor.

"Simon Purslip," I repeated slowly. "The Long-Fingered Man." Then I stopped talking, just like Matt always did.

"Who's he?" Alex asked.

"He's not real, dummy," Kyle said. "It's only a story."

"That's what I thought at first, too." Then I told him just what Matt had said. "It doesn't matter if you believe me or not. It's true."

"He's realer than the Squeaking Skull," Alex said.

Everyone giggled.

Except Kyle. "Whatever," he said.

"Go ahead, Charlie," Joey said. "Why do they call him that?"

"Simon Purslip had long, skinny hands," I whispered. I held up my hands in the dark and wiggled my fingers in front of the flashlight. "On each hand he had six fingers, not five. And his index fingers were *twelve inches long*."

"A whole foot long!" Alex exclaimed.

I kept going. I couldn't remember exactly what Matt had said, so I just made some things up. "Simon Purslip had lived in that house for fifty years. No one knew how he came to be there. And no one saw him during the day. The Long-Fingered Man had all his food and everything delivered to the back door of his house, and no one ever saw him take it in."

"Then how do they know there even was a long-fingered man?" asked Kyle. He didn't sound quite so bossy now.

"Because every so often people saw him at night." Then, just like Matt, I paused and waited in silence.

"Who saw him?" Joey asked. Now he had his pillow over his head.

"At first just grown-ups. Grown-ups who were out late at night. They'd be walking their dogs, or just going down to the late-night store on Central Avenue."

"I know where that is!" Alex said.

"And people would say they saw this really, really thin man walking down the street. He had this long coat and sticking out of the sleeves"—I held up my fingers in the air and waggled them slowly, just like Matt did—"were these really long, bony fingers... reeealllly long...bony...fingers."

While I was talking, I saw Tommy slip out of his sleeping bag and tiptoe out of the room. Nobody else seemed to notice. Maybe he wanted to peel more of the glue off his face, or maybe he just needed to go to the bathroom.

I kept going, and the story got scarier. I told them about pets and other animals disappearing. I was afraid I might scare myself.

Alex was sitting up on his sleeping bag. His knee was jiggling up and down a little, but the rest of him was very still, which was a miracle for Alex.

"Then, one night, someone who had seen the Long-Fingered Man went out for a walk. But he didn't come back."

"How do they know?" Kyle asked.

"His wife called the police," I said.

"Oh," Kyle said. I could see his face by the hall light. He seemed kind of worried.

"They looked high and low for him," I said, "but they never found him."

"Why didn't they ask the Long-Fingered Man?" Joey asked.

"The police went to his door and knocked. He told them he didn't know anything about it. And they believed him."

"Stupid police," Joey said.

"Really stupid," Alex said. I looked at Hector. He had a smile on his face. He was loving the story!

"And then, one by one, more and more people disappeared. First, it was just grown-ups. And their pets, if they were walking them. It happened over a long period of time, so that in between people kind of forgot about it."

"Dumb grown-ups," Joey said.

"And then, finally, one day, there was this kid. My brother said his name was Jason, and he lived on Turner Drive."

"What?" Alex gasped. "That's *this* street!"

"Really?" Joey looked like he might swallow his sleeping bag.

I saw Kyle glance toward the window.

"I know," I said. "And he was in fifth grade."

"At King Philip?" Joey said. "He went to *our* school?"

"Uh-huh," I said. "And one night, he let his dog out to go to the bathroom, and when the dog didn't come back, Jason went outside to look for him."

"Oh no," Alex whispered.

"Right," I said. "So he went down to the end of the driveway and he looked up and down the street. And then, he thought he saw something standing behind a tree."

"This isn't true," Kyle said. But he didn't say it like he didn't believe it. He said it like he was afraid it was true and didn't want it to be.

"But what if it is?" Hector asked. He was totally into the story.

I wondered why Tommy hadn't come back. Maybe he'd changed his mind about listening to scary stories. I decided to finish up quickly.

"So, the kid, Jason, started to walk over to the tree to see what it was, and then out from behind the tree came...the Long...Fingered...Man!" I whispered. Everyone leaned closer. I looked around. Kyle's eyes were open wide. Joey had a pillow over his face. And then, I saw Tommy creeping into the room behind Joey, Alex, and Kyle with his arms spread out. He was wearing Hector's mask and he was going to scare everyone's pants off.

The attack of the chupacabra!

"NOOOOOOOOOOO!" I screamed at him. At the same time he let out a bloodcurdling yell. "AAAAAAAAAAHHH!"

And then everyone else screamed in terror, "AAAAAAAAAAAAAAHHH!"

They were completely freaked out.

Except for Hector, who fell over on his side laughing.

"It's only Tommy!" I yelled.

But Tommy kept on screeching and jumping on one kid after another. Maybe he couldn't tell that they were really scared.

"Tommy, stop it! Stop it!" I grabbed him and pulled off the chupacabra mask.

Joey and Alex were still screaming.

"Omigod!" Alex yelled. "You almost made me wet my pants!" Then he started laughing.

"I want my mommy!" Joey shouted. But he started to laugh, too. Hector was laughing so hard he had tears in his eyes.

I looked over at Kyle. He was just sitting on his sleeping bag, rocking back and forth.

"Are you okay?" I asked him.

"Shut up," he said. "Leave me alone."

Tommy was still jumping around, making horror sounds.

"Hey, Tommy," I said. "Cut it out."

Just then, the overhead lights in the family room came on.

"What's going on here?" Mr. McLeod asked. He was one unhappy-looking grown-up.

"Um…Charlie told a ghost story and Tommy scared us and…" Alex seemed to run out of explanations.

"Okay," his dad said. "That's enough. It's late. You guys need to get in your sleeping bags and go to sleep. Absolutely no more noise. Don't make me come down here again."

While Mr. McLeod was talking, Kyle had rolled up his sleeping bag. He picked it up and went over to the corner and put on his sneakers.

"What's wrong, Kyle?" Alex's dad asked.

"Nothing," Kyle said.

"What are you doing?"

"Going home," he said. "I have a stomachache."

We all got really quiet when he said that. I could tell he didn't want to talk about it and was trying to get out as quickly as he could.

"Do you want me to walk you home?" Alex's dad said.

"No," Kyle said. "My mom said she'd leave the back door open."

"Uh-oh," Joey said. "She must not have known about the Long-Fingered Man."

I saw the look on Kyle's face when Joey said that.

"Come on. I'll walk you home," Alex's dad said.

"Okay," Kyle said.

"Hey, Kyle, don't you want your movie?" Alex asked.

"I'll get it later," he mumbled.

"Okay, good night," Alex said.

"Good night," Kyle said.

"Good night, Kyle," we all said back.

Then he left with Alex's dad, who was still just wearing his bathrobe and slippers.

We all sat around in a circle in our sleeping bags.

"Kyle wasn't sick," Joey said. "He was scared. That's why he went home."

"He said he wasn't going to be scared," Tommy said. "But he was the most scared of all of us."

"He's really a chicken," Alex said.

"Wait until people hear about that! Kyle Curtis is a scaredy cat!" Joey said. "He kept talking about the Shrieking Skull, but he couldn't stand to hear about the Long-Fingered Man."

"And the chupacabra finished him off!" Tommy added.

"It was pretty funny," Alex said.

"Not really," I said.

"Yes, it was," Hector said. "Your story was very funny."

"I know," I said. "And it *was* kind of funny for Tommy to jump out like that. But still—"

"It was hilarious, Charlie," Alex said. "And you taught Kyle a lesson—he said he wasn't scared of anything. But he was."

"I don't know," I said. "I don't like being scared. Kyle was right. I never wanted to see *The Shrieking Skull*, but I was afraid to say so. And I don't like scaring people, either."

Then we sat there for about ten seconds not saying anything. I sort of wished I hadn't said all that. But it was true.

"I think it's okay," Tommy said.

"Me, too," said Alex.

"I guess this means we can't watch *The Shrieking Skull*," Joey said.

"You mean the squeaking skull?" Tommy said. "Eeek-eeek!"

Then we all started squeaking like mice. And we started jumping on each other, eeking and squeaking and pretending we were going to eat each other alive.

Alex's dad came back in the house. "Hey! Quiet down, all of you!" he said. "Go to sleep!"

And we did.

24

The Squid Delivers

The next morning, Alex's parents made us pancakes.

Mom picked me up around ten o'clock. I was pretty tired when I got in the car.

"Did you have fun?" Mom asked.

"Uh-huh," I said.

"Did you get a lot of candy?"

"Nope," I said. "Hardly any."

"Why not?" she asked.

"We didn't get to go to very many houses," I muttered. "And it seemed like the bigger the house, the smaller the candy bars. It was the least candy I ever got."

"Hmmm," Mom said. Then she drove for a while without saying anything.

I looked out the window. "Did Mabel get a lot of candy?" I asked.

"She did pretty well," Mom said. "She wanted to come with me to pick you up, but I had some errands to do first, so she stayed home. She's waiting for you."

"Probably to show off her candy," I grumbled.

"Probably," Mom said. "Did you watch a movie?"

"Yeah," I said. "*Space Gremlins.* Remember when we saw it?"

"I think so. Was it scary?"

"Not really," I said.

"So you were okay?" she asked. "Nothing too horrifying?"

"No. Not at all," I said. That was all I wanted to say—I didn't want to talk about the Long-Fingered Man.

◆ ◆ ◆

When we turned into the driveway, Matt was shooting baskets. Mom got out of the car and went in the house.

"Hey, Chickenmeister!" Matt said. "Did you freak out?"

"No," I said.

"I told you. The Long-Fingered Man did his job."

"I hate the Long-Fingered Man," I said.

"That's okay. He still did his job," Matt said, dribbling the ball back and forth.

"Did you scare anybody?" I asked.

"Just Jared," Matt said. "He screamed his butt off."

I wished I could have seen that.

"The only problem was he had his little brother with him, and I scared him, too. Mom made me call up their parents and apologize."

I smiled at him, and he gave me his evil older brother smile right back.

Matt bounced the ball a couple of times. "Did you have fun?"

I thought about that. Matt was really asking me like he was an older brother who wanted to know, not an older brother who wanted to prove I was an idiot.

"It was okay," I said. "But I like it better around here."

Matt smirked and shot a basket. "That's because I'm here."

I didn't tell him he was partly right.

"Charlie!" The Squid was standing at the back door holding a big grocery bag. "Look what I have!"

"I know what it is, Squid," I said. "I don't want to see it."

"Yes, you do," she said. "It's a lot!"

"I know it's a lot. Don't rub it in. I don't want to see all your candy."

"It's not mine."

"What do you mean?" I asked.

"Mine's in my room," she said. "I counted it all up and there are eighty-seven pieces. This is yours!"

"What do you mean?"

"I told people that my brother couldn't come trick-or-treating with me and I wanted to surprise him. I took along an extra bag, so everybody gave me some extra candy for you. This is for you, so you're not mad about Brady being the rabbit bat."

My mouth opened but no words came out. I couldn't believe it. I walked up the steps and looked in the bag. It was filled with candy.

"Wow, Mabel," I mumbled. "Thanks a lot."

"You're welcome," she said with a huge grin that showed her two new front teeth.

Matt came over and looked in. "Whoa," he said. "The Squid delivers."

"I know," I said.

"Are you still mad?" the Squid asked.

I shook my head. I wasn't mad.

I had survived Halloween. And the Shrieking
Skull.

And I had tons of candy.

And that was pretty good.

Don't miss the other books
in the Charlie Bumpers series—
Charlie Bumpers vs. the Teacher of the Year,
Charlie Bumpers vs. the Really Nice Gnome, and
Charlie Bumpers vs. the Perfect Little Turkey.
Also available as audio books.

*And watch for the fifth book
in the series, coming up soon!*

HC: 978-1-56145-732-8
PB: 978-1-56145-824-0
CD: 978-1-56145-770-0

HC: 978-1-56145-740-3
PB: 978-1-56145-831-8
CD: 978-1-56145-788-5

HC: 978-1-56145-835-6
CD: 978-1-56145-893-6

BILL HARLEY is the author of the award-winning middle reader novels *The Amazing Flight of Darius Frobisher* and *Night of the Spadefoot Toads*. He is also a storyteller, musician, and writer who has been writing and performing for kids and families for more than twenty years. Harley is the recipient of Parents' Choice and ALA awards, as well as two Grammy Awards. He lives in Massachusetts.

www.billharley.com

ADAM GUSTAVSON has illustrated many books for children, including *Lost and Found*; *The Blue House Dog*; *Mind Your Manners, Alice Roosevelt!*; and *Snow Day!* He lives in New Jersey.

www.adamgustavson.com